Desert Hunt

*A prequel to the
Wolves of Twin Moon Ranch
series*

by Anna Lowe

Copyright © 2015 Anna Lowe

All rights reserved.

Editing by Lisa A. Hollett

Covert art by Fiona Jayde Media
www.FionaJaydeMedia.com

Contents

Contents	i
Other books in this series	iii
Free Book	v
Prologue	1
Chapter One	5
Chapter Two	9
Chapter Three	15
Chapter Four	19
Chapter Five	25
Chapter Six	31
Chapter Seven	41
Chapter Eight	49
Chapter Nine	53
Chapter Ten	57
Chapter Eleven	63

Chapter Twelve	69
Chapter Thirteen	73
Chapter Fourteen	79
Chapter Fifteen	87
Chapter Sixteen	95
Chapter Seventeen	99
Chapter Eighteen	105
Chapter Nineteen	111
Chapter Twenty	115
Chapter Twenty-One	121
Chapter Twenty-Two	127
Chapter Twenty-Three	133
Chapter Twenty-Four	135
Chapter Twenty-Five	139
Epilogue	143
Sneak Peek I: Desert Moon	149
Sneak Peek II: Desert Moon	151
Other books by Anna Lowe	155
More from Anna Lowe	157
About the Author	159

Other books in this series

Desert Hunt (the Prequel)

Desert Moon (Book 1)

Desert Wolf 1 (a short story)

Desert Wolf 2 (a short story)

Desert Wolf 3 (a short story)

Desert Blood (Book 2)

Desert Fate (Book 3)

Desert Heart (Book 4)

Happily Mated After (a short story)

Desert Yule (a short story)

Desert Rose (Book 5)

Desert Roots (Book 6)

visit www.annalowebooks.com

Free Book

Desert Wolf

Get your free e-book now!

Sign up for my newsletter at *annalowebooks.com* to get your free copy of *Desert Wolf: Friend or Foe* (Book 1.1 in the series).

Lana Dixon may have won her destined mate's heart, but that was in Arizona. Now, she's bringing her desert wolf home to meet her family — the sworn enemies of his pack. How far will they push her mate to prove himself worthy? And is their relationship ready for the test?

Prologue

"Rae!"

It was a barked order, not a request.

Rae gritted her teeth and counted to five before turning slowly and facing the source: Sabrina, the daughter of the wolf pack's ruling alpha. The girl was seventeen and still a spoiled brat. Rae didn't want to imagine what the girl might be like in another couple of years.

"My father wants you in his office. Now." Sabrina underpinned the command with a flick of her glossy mane.

Rae wouldn't have thought it possible for a wolf shifter to be a princess, but there it was. Sabrina made damn sure she punctuated every sentence with a jangle of gold bracelets and the same two words—*my father*—reminding everyone of the pecking order around here.

That was one of the bitter truths of pack hierarchy. The alphas and their offspring ruled the roost, and the rest of the pack had no choice but to fight or submit. Twenty-eight hardscrabble years had taught Rae that all too well.

She chipped another little piece off her soul and did as directed, pretending to be like the others. A good little female meant for hearth and home—and definitely, definitely, not for the hunt.

She worked off the tension steeling her jaw, reminding herself she had something far, far more special in her heritage than alpha blood. Something secret. But she'd be damned if she let on to anyone. A pack would claim her forever if they found out, and then she'd never be free.

"Do you ever bother looking in a mirror?" Sabrina eyed Rae's tangled hair.

Not nearly as often as you. Rae nearly shot the words out but caught herself on the first syllable. So what if her long brown hair was usually thrown into a loose ponytail? So what if her figure said *athlete* and not *cover girl*? That's who she was, and she liked it that way. She'd leave the plunging necklines to curvy girls like Sabrina, because attracting unwanted attention could be a dangerous thing.

She set off, finger-combing her hair on the way to the alpha's office and flicking away a burr she'd picked up that morning. So she'd been out wandering again. Was that so wrong for one of their kind?

Except she wasn't exactly their kind. Oh, she was a wolf shifter all right, but one born to another pack. And even back home in Colorado, she'd always been different. The one who didn't quite fit in.

Her inner wolf let out a snort. *A lot different. If only they knew.*

Rae eyed the alpha's office door warily before giving it a nervous knock. There was a grunt, and she entered, dropping her eyes in the required sign of subordination to the grizzled old alpha and his haughty mate. Even after all these years at Westend pack, the gesture didn't come easily.

"Your lucky day has come," Roric announced, curt and cold. "Pack your things."

For this alpha, a smile and a sneer were one and the same. What did he mean by *lucky day?*

Rae glanced uncertainly at Roric's mate, who frowned in acid disapproval of Rae's dusty jeans, her plain blue T-shirt, her... Well, her everything.

"Get moving." Roric jutted his square chin toward the door. "Another pack is willing to try you out for a season."

Rae's heart thumped. She'd been hoping something would come along in another pack—a job, an internship, anything. She'd had enough of Nevada. Not so much the heat or the dusty flats but the stifling hierarchy of Roric's Westend pack. That and the fact that these shifters had sold their souls. Gambling was big business in Nevada, but as far as Rae was concerned, it was a business wolf packs had no place in. What happened to their connection to the earth, to the old ways?

Unfortunately, Roric's pack had only let go of *some* of the old ways. They'd clung to the rest: the crushing, absolutist authority, the strict delineation of male and female roles. The only consolation was that Roric wasn't as bad as some others—like the alpha Rae had fled in Colorado ten years earlier. Here, her body was safe. And by now, she'd learned the ropes. If she toed the line carefully, she had a modicum of freedom. After all, no one ever paid attention to what the odd wolf out did on the night of a new moon.

But who knew what it would be like in a different pack?

"Where?" she blurted.

Roric waved a lazy hand as if it were all the same to him. But that gesture, like so many others, was probably rehearsed. The alpha didn't do anything without analyzing it for the benefits—to him and his pack. Individual wishes didn't register on his list.

"Arizona. Twin Moon Ranch."

She caught a breath. When she'd put in a request for a transfer, she'd been thinking East Coast, where the packs were said to be more modern-minded. But Arizona? Wolf packs in the Four Corners area were known to be old school. And Arizona—that was old-old school. Who knew what kind of alpha she'd have there?

She glanced around, second-guessing herself. Westend had never felt like home, but did she really want to start all over again?

The hard faces greeting her provided all the answer she needed: the decision was made.

"Who knows," the alpha female added with a conspiratorial glance at her partner. "You might finally find a suitable mate there."

Rae hid the stutter in her breath. Was that a hint? A threat? The room leaned in over her, as enclosed spaces always did. She let her chin dip into the briefest nod, asking—begging—to be dismissed while her mind spun. *Arizona?*

Roric flicked a finger toward the door. She was released.

"Good luck," Sabrina called, her tone clashing with the words.

Right, luck. Rae had been in Nevada long enough to know that it took a hell of a lot of waiting to win at any gamble. Better to make her own luck, or at least stack the odds in her favor.

She hurried to her room, forcing calm over her mind as she decided which of her few belongings mattered enough to take. Topping the list was her recurve bow and a freshly fletched set of arrows, with a few silver-tipped ones, just in case. Because there were wolves, and there were *wolves*. Who knew what Arizona might bring?

Chapter One

Zack stretched and squinted into the morning sun. He took a deep, testing breath and got a lungful of promise. He did it again, just to be sure. No, he hadn't been dreaming. The desert really was alive with an enticing new scent. One of those fresh, optimistic scents that said spring was coming and everything would be new, good, and clean. He'd gotten home late last night after a week away tracking, but the scent had struck him the minute he rolled his Harley back onto the ranch. Something like the fragrance of a century plant in bloom— something that didn't come along but once in a very long time.

He looked around, searching for the first hints of spring as he walked the meandering path that connected his hermit's cabin to the bustling central part of the ranch. But nothing was blooming, at least not yet. The ocotillo weren't showing any scarlet buds, nor were the manzanitas giving any hint of color.

So what the hell was that scent?

He sniffed again, figuring it was one of those tricks of nature. The desert was full of mirages that showed a man what he wanted to see, only to cackle and whisk them away. For all that his Navajo mother had tried instilling the beauty of nature in him, his white father's skeptical nature seemed to win out. The desert was simply another place on earth—just emptier, quieter, and more dangerous than the rest.

He wound around the ranch outbuildings, heading for the work shed. A tracker's job was an on-and-off gig that he balanced with projects on the ranch. This past week, he'd been tracking trespassers on the north edge of pack territory. A gang of three, it seemed, who'd long since come and gone. Nothing to worry about.

Today seemed like a normal morning on the ranch with the usual guys out on the usual jobs. Except that Ty, the pack's second-in-command, was over there, looking like a thundercloud that had stalled on a craggy mountain peak. Zack pulled up in midstep, wondering what was wrong. Ty was hacking at the earth like it was his mortal enemy.

"Hey," Zack called by way of greeting. He walked up and steadied the fence post while Ty chopped the earth around it in short, angry swipes.

"Hey," Ty grunted without looking up.

For Ty, that passed for warm and fuzzy. Anyone but Zack, his oldest friend, would have earned an outright growl.

The funny thing was, they had no business being friends. They'd both known it, even as kids. As the alpha's oldest son, Ty couldn't mix with just anyone and neither could the no-good half-breed from out on the western fringe of the ranch. Yet somehow, that was enough to bond them in spite of the odds.

"You okay?" Zack ventured, watching Ty hack away.

"Sure. Good."

Zack lifted an eyebrow but kept his mouth shut. He sighed and found himself savoring the air. That scent was stronger down here on the ranch. A scent that tempted him to hope for something better in life. He bent his head against it, concentrating on his work. Hope only led to disappointment—a lesson he'd learned young and hard.

Of course, that lesson only held true for some people. Hope sure seemed to work for people like Ty's younger brother Cody, who was walking by now, chipper as always.

"Heya, Zack! Ty!"

Zack gave him a nod. Yes, optimism worked if you were the younger son of an alpha and life laid a golden path before your feet. Light on responsibility but heavy on privilege.

Ty straightened, bringing his six-foot-two frame eye to eye with Zack's. As the oldest son and heir apparent, Ty had it the other way around: heavy on responsibility, light on privilege.

These days, his intense eyes pretended he was more machine than man, but Zack knew the truth. Inside was a man yearning to breathe free.

Funny how two friends could be so different, yet so very much alike.

Working and sweating side by side... They hadn't done that in a while, and it felt good. Zack could forget he was the son of a vagrant wolf and a coyote mother, and Ty could pretend he could take on the whole world all by himself.

"You got it?" Ty murmured.

"Got it."

They switched places, Ty bracing the post while Zack excavated. He couldn't resist another long drag of that air. Might as well enjoy it while it lasted. That scent was full of color and life and... Damn it, there it was again: promise.

A dog huffed in the distance, and a woman turned the corner at the very same moment that the desert expunged another breath of that sweet, clear air. Zack watched her glide by with an easy, graceful step, and his wolf gave an appreciative whistle before launching into one of his inner monologues.

Bet she could run for miles.

Yeah, she probably could.

Bet she could scale the hills without losing her breath.

That, too.

Bet she could lead a wolf on a chase to remember...

He slammed the brakes on there and gave his head a firm shake.

"Check it out," one of the ranch hands whispered to another. Zack's keen ears caught every word. "The new girl."

"Yeah, welcome to the ranch, sweetheart," the other ranch hand said, not loud enough for her to hear.

Zack's inner wolf growled.

With that windswept almond hair and lanky limbs, she was much, much too appealing for her own good. The defiant jut of her chin wasn't for show; this was a woman ready to defend her cause, whatever it was. Pretty and totally unafraid. A dangerous combination for an unclaimed female away from her home turf.

Zack followed her movements much longer and closer than he'd intended. Everything about her said wild, tangled, and free. Everything he wanted to be.

A dozen pairs of eyes trailed after her as she strode across the work yard, with one strap of her overalls loose, the other tight. A new female on the ranch was always cause for speculation, and a colt-legged, sharp-eyed country girl like this scored highest of all. And from the looks of it, *score* was on every man's mind.

He tested the air. She was a shifter, all right. He could sense the wolf in her, see the self-control holding the beast in check. It was right there, under the surface—closer than most females shifters allowed their wolves, as if she was on guard. The question was, on guard against what?

Not your type, part of his brain ordered. *Definitely not your type.*

Just my type, his wolf growled.

Exactly my type, his coyote agreed.

That's what he got for being a mixed-breed: two voices in his head, even if he only ever shifted into the same canine body—big as a wolf with the dun-colored coat and pointed muzzle of a coyote. But the voices were always separate inside, and the wolf and coyote parts of his brain rarely agreed.

We agree on her, both chuckled at the same time.

Chapter Two

Zack watched a dog run up to the new girl, putting on a snarling show. But she stopped it with a single firm syllable. Within a minute, she'd turned the vicious mutt into a leg-thumping puddle of mush. Half the guys in sight looked like they'd be ready to do the same until a harsh whisper broke the mood.

"Crap! Look."

"Quick. He's coming."

Everyone scrambled back to work as the sound of booted feet stalked into the yard. Old Tyrone, senior alpha of the pack, was approaching, and everybody went on high alert. Zack's shoulders tensed and he gripped the post tighter. Ty did, too; he could sense it.

The alpha stomped right up to Zack, clamped a viselike hand over the back of his neck, and squeezed. Zack held his breath and stood very, very still. From a distance, the older man's gesture might pass for a wise old alpha leaning in to give a young up-and-comer a word of well-meaning advice.

Something like, *Doing good, son?*

As if the old man had ever taken the time to give him words like that.

Good job on the last tracking assignment.

That would be like a foreign language, though. The only praise he'd ever gotten came from soothing female voices like Aunt Jean's, or his mother's, a long time ago.

But this was old Tyrone, and his grip was a threat. A warning.

My son will be alpha of this pack someday. That's what the gesture said. *You, boy, are nothing. You never will be. Dare to think otherwise and I will snap your dirty neck.*

As a kid, it had been terrifying.

As an adult, it should have been laughable. Zack had done a lot of growing since then, topping out a good two inches over the alpha. He could take on the grizzled old man if he wanted. But why would he want to? He would never do anything that might threaten the stability of his pack.

He shrugged out of the hold. What was the old man warning him off now? The woman? He could have snorted. All he wanted was to finish the day's work so he could get out in the open and find whatever it was that was tickling him inside. That scent—everything in him screamed to track it down until he knew it, understood it, rubbed himself in it. To possess even a tiny part of it.

His coyote sniffed the air, considering. *That scent is nice. New.*

Mine, the wolf snarled.

Zack stood quietly, willing Tyrone away.

The old man rolled his knuckles until they cracked, waiting for Zack to submit. Except submissive wasn't in Zack's blood, and they both knew it.

He wished the old alpha would just get it. Was he a born alpha? Yes. Did he have to challenge pack leadership to prove it? No. All he wanted was his own space, and out on the periphery was fine with him. He'd never do anything to the detriment of the pack. Never. Why couldn't the old man get that?

Back off, old man, Zack's wolf snarled inside, though he held perfectly still.

It was Ty who broke the impasse by clearing his throat—turning the old man's ire on him.

"You talk to her yet?" the old alpha growled at his son.

Zack nearly answered. *Not yet.* Because it felt like he ought to have talked to the woman, or he already had. Like he somehow knew her, or they'd met before.

But the question wasn't directed at him. It was aimed at Ty, who let a second tick by before answering.

"Not yet." His voice was so low, it could have been a rumble from behind the hills.

"When then?"

What the hell was that all about?

"When I decide," Ty growled back.

"There's nothing to decide. Just do it," the old man ordered.

Zack had to wonder what was worse: having an absent bastard of a father, like his own, or an all-too-present bastard of a father, like Ty's. The old man was always there, looking over his son's shoulder. Over everyone else's, too.

Old Tyrone aimed another glare of warning at Zack—who stared back—before releasing a regal grunt and moving away.

Another minute ticked by before either Zack or Ty released a breath. Ty scratched at his ear and drilled his heel into the ground, suddenly weary.

"The new girl, Rae..." he started.

Zack glanced at the retreating figure as the letters rollercoastered through his mind. Rae. A name for the face already imprinted on his memory. Something rumbled low in his gut before she turned a corner and disappeared, taking the breeze of promise with her.

Two of the younger ranch hands strode purposefully after her, only to suddenly divert under Tyrone's withering glare.

"Make sure none of the guys mess around with her," Ty finished, his voice grim.

Zack barely arrested the sharp swivel of his head. What did Ty care for the newcomer?

He hazarded a covert sniff of his friend. A second sniff confirmed the first: there wasn't a trace of lust on the alpha-in-waiting. Ty hadn't shown sincere interest in any woman for years—at least, no interest in anything more than a quick romp and roll. The local girls threw themselves at him like a herd of lovesick broodmares but rarely lucked out, unless Ty's wolf decided to sample the offerings. His human side was more restrained and had been for years. Ever since the time he'd come home from a trip and gone half out of his mind, searching for a mate that didn't exist.

And there it was: proof that the desert was full of tricks. If Ty—unmovable, unassailable Ty—could be thrown into a tailspin over a mystery scent, then Zack should be on guard, too.

He willed his nostrils to stop testing the air as he covertly regarded his friend. If it wasn't lust, why did Ty care about the woman? The only emotion he could pick up in Ty was a platonic kind of protectiveness, the kind he showed around any man who had the nerve to prowl too close to his sisters. Maybe Rae was a distant cousin or something. Maybe that's why old Tyrone pushed Zack away.

"We need a new post-hole digger," Ty grumbled as the tool snapped with a rusty crunch. "Damn thing's broken."

"How broken?" Zack used a familiar old line from their childhood to ease some of the tension.

Ty didn't smile, but his head bobbed. "Broken enough."

Part of Zack wanted to go back to those more innocent days, while another part knew it was no good. Nothing would change the way things were now.

"Got it." He nodded back and set off for the tool shed, crossing the open space in a couple of long strides.

Even before he turned the corner to the shed, his ears picked up the sound of jangling bells, low moos, and sharp whistles. The cattle were being herded to the stock pens.

He cleared the turn and saw a hundred head coming his way. In a minute, they'd be at the narrow neck between the barn and a long row of sheds. He let out an impatient breath and moved aside. There was no way through until the cattle funneled out.

They swept toward him, lowing and huffing, kicking up a cloud of dust that threatened to consume a figure in front of him. It was the new girl—woman, he corrected himself; despite her tomboy look, everything about her screamed hot-blooded woman—moving out of their path. Step by step, she backed up to the line of sheds. Another step, and she was right in front of Zack, still blind to his presence. One more, and his hands went up in warning just as she pressed into him, her back to his front.

Warm, was all his mind registered at first.

Tight, his fingers added, feeling the muscles wrapped around her middle like a corset.

Sweet, his body hummed, picking up her scent.

Mine, his wolf growled, starting to pace inside the mental cage Zack had constructed around that side of his being.

Because the scent that had him on tenterhooks all morning wasn't washing in from the open desert. It was coming from her. It *was* her.

Something in her called to him—to a deep, primal part that didn't know the meaning of no.

"Gotcha," he half-whispered, half-growled.

His ears filled with the ringing of more than just the cowbells. It was an internal alarm triggered as she squeezed even closer, her tight rear setting off fireworks in his groin. The fine line of her back curved into his chest in a custom fit, and his thoughts shattered into a hundred chopped-up syllables.

Mine! Mate! the wolf growled.

The human part wasn't much better. *Holy. Shit.*

The coyote, he just laughed.

They stood plastered together while his heart sounded with the solemn stroke of a grandfather clock, somewhere far, far down the imaginary hallway of his mind. Low, resounding strokes separated by pregnant pauses.

Bong. He sucked in a long, shallow breath, trying to clear his mind. *Bong.* Was it nearly midnight, the party about to end? *Bong.* Jesus, how could it be? The very woman Ty asked him to protect was the first to ever to penetrate this deep into his soul.

Bong.

Trouble, sure trouble, on the way.

Chapter Three

Rae had been so engrossed in thought that she'd come face to face with a couple of thousand pounds of beef on the hoof. Here she'd been thinking about which people to watch out for on the ranch when it seemed livestock was the greater threat.

She started backing away from the oncoming herd, trying to settle her mind. Maybe she was being too wary, trying to judge her new pack. Everyone seemed welcoming enough, and if some of the men were a bit too welcoming, well, that was to be expected in a den of wolves.

Still, she wasn't ready to let her guard down and accept that she'd lucked out with a good pack. Not just yet. For all that she'd had a good start at Twin Moon, there was a weird vibe in the way some people treated her. Not everyone, but a select few. Like the old alpha, who watched her come and go like a man judging a panel of job applicants. A ranch hand like her shouldn't merit the attention of the alpha. Meanwhile, his older son avoided her like the plague, and though the younger son, Cody, had come on strong in their first meeting, he'd done an about-face and backed right off since then.

Either she was imagining things, or something was going on. Something she couldn't make head or tail of.

Then again, maybe she was too used to searching for ulterior motives. The people here seemed honest and sincere. That or they were doing a damn good job of tricking her into a false sense of security.

She'd been tricked before. In life, in love. And she damn sure wasn't going to fall victim again. So she kept her guard up, just in case.

Except she hadn't kept enough of it up to avoid walking straight into the cattle. To make matters worse, now she'd gone and backed into a mountain of living, breathing flesh.

Man-flesh.

Melted into him was more like it, because the minute they made contact, her bones went molten, her muscles turning to mush instead of jumping away when she realized that she'd parked herself right on top of a stranger.

On top of, her wolf breathed, a little giddy. *Not a bad idea...*

Apparently his wolf was on the same wavelength because she could feel an unmistakable hardening against her lower back as he hummed into her ear.

"Gotcha."

Two choppy syllables that promised more than just a snug fit in his arms.

Her inner wolf all but purred. *Got me, for sure.*

She batted at the beast, ordering it to behave.

Don't be such a prude, the wolf complained.

Don't be such a hussy, she hissed back.

His hand slid along her spine, sending uneven shots of heat to her core. For all that she wanted to stick an elbow in the ribs of the stranger who dared press up against her like that, she found herself pressing back. Inhaling. Enjoying, almost.

If he'd said one more word or leaned half an inch closer, she might have shoved him away. But his stunned silence told her his reaction was just as involuntary as hers. So she stood still, basking in his presence.

Damn cattle. She tried off-loading the blame.

The herd lumbered on, jostling and complaining, oblivious of their crime.

He wants us like we want him, her wolf hummed, smug.

Rae shook head firmly even as her soul heated under his touch. *Jed wanted us, too. Remember him? Remember how close we nearly came to—*

Her wolf snarled, cutting her off. *Jed was a mistake.*

A mistake we won't repeat.

The beast howled. *A wolf needs a mate!*

Rae stiffened. Mate? Where the hell did that come from?

He's ours. Don't you know the scent of your destined mate?

She could barely tell if the thumping in her chest came from her heart or his. *Destiny plays tricks, all the time. We make mistakes.*

This is no mistake! The howl turned to a scream as the pressure against her ribs increased. Her wolf was trying to get out.

She pushed the beast back into her inner cage. The man behind her, though, was impossible to ignore.

He was big, that much was clear. Half a head taller than her, judging by the angle of his minty breath on her ear. Broad, like his shadow. Blissfully warm and somehow soft for all the slabs of muscle plastered over his frame. Layer upon layer of it that slid and groaned over each another like so many tectonic plates.

The herd lumbered closer, and a panicked corner of her mind was thinking of climbing the fence to get away from it all: the dust, the cattle, the man. Between the space of one breath and the next, though, the man whipped out from behind her and took up guard in front, forming a solid wall between her and the livestock. And just like that, Rae found herself in a little bubble of calm, listening to her heart thump.

Whistles and alarms went off in her mind, but her wolf just purred in pleasure, canting her hips forward. *Damn perfect ass...*

She couldn't resist going up on tiptoe and nosing closer to his neck to inhale a deep breath of his musk. He was fresh, smooth, and edgy all at the same time, like a man who washed in a mountain stream and slept naked with the covers off. The wolf musk was there along with something foreign—something earthy, scruffy, and wild. Her errant fingers ran up his back and brushed the curly bottom edge of his hair that barely cleared the collar of his cotton work shirt. His hair was thick and wavy and satchel brown, though the sun-drenched tips were dun-colored, like... like... coyote?

Rae's nostrils flared as her nose continued its inspection. Apparently, the he-wolf had a splash of coyote in him. That was unusual. The human part of him was just as hard to decipher. The lemony smell of honesty was in there, mixed in with the chili-laced scent of regret. He turned slowly with a look that dared a thousand head of cattle to break past the barrier he made.

She looked up at green-brown eyes filled with the residue of a stormy past. Hurt and loneliness were in there, overwritten with a fierce sense of pride and honor. Hope, too—a faint glimmer of it, like the first star at twilight.

"You okay?" he whispered.

She took in the parentheses around his mouth, the chunks of muscle on his arms. His left arm boxed in her waist, while his right arm reached up past her shoulder to grip the fence behind her. She could have ducked out any time, yet she remained rooted to the spot, listening to her own uneven breath.

"Perfect," she murmured.

Vaguely, she registered that the cattle were gone, and it was just him and her, standing impossibly close. Her lips moved a little more, though she failed to produce any sound.

The man watched, waiting, with his head tilted as if a rare songbird were singing and he needed to catch every fleeting note. She could smell his arousal, feel the cool of the first layer of morning sweat breaking from his body. A tip of her chin and their lips would line up—

A dog barked at the heels of one last cow, jolting her back to rational thought and a less brazen pose. Another minute and she'd have her ankle wound around his calf. Who was this man? And how could he have such an effect on her?

Her wolf heaved a dreamy sigh. *Mate.*

Then it was his turn to blink and snap to, breaking whatever spell had been cast over the two of them. His forehead folded into a hundred anxious creases as he sidestepped away, murmuring incoherently. Was he apologizing? Aghast at her brazenness? Turned on?

Maybe all three. Rae couldn't tell. Only that he was gone the next instant, and she was alone.

Chapter Four

Zack decided to blame his oversensitivity to the new woman on the full moon. He could feel it rising—once the buzzing in his ears settled down, that is. Yeah, he'd blame that on the moon, along with the tightness in his jeans and the sweat breaking out on his brow. The man who could run a full day and night through the desert was winded by a lightweight. A woman.

Damn, but she'd brought something out in him.

He hastily corrected himself. It was the full moon. It had to be. Because why else was he trying to hang on to the feel of her in his arms? Why else would the scent of her make it hard to walk a straight line, even after hours had gone by?

"Coming out tonight, Zack, honey?" a sugar-sweet voice called, full of thinly veiled promise.

Hell, no. Zack barely bit back the comment as he turned to face Audrey.

Dear God, what was the woman wearing today? Some kind of pink frou-frou thing that barely covered her nipples, let alone the rest of her breasts. Which, he supposed, was the point. The self-styled playgirl of the ranch had her role down to the hilt, from the highlighted tips of her overbleached hair to the ruby-red lips that shaped words like, *Here. Now. Me.*

He backed away. Yeah, he'd played around with Audrey a couple of times—or had gotten played by her. Hell, every man on the ranch had, but whatever the appeal had once been, it just wasn't there any more. Besides, he was tired of being second or third choice.

"Lemme guess," he offered, resuming his swinging stride as Audrey hurried alongside. "Ty's busy tonight. Cody, too."

Everyone on the ranch knew how the singles scene worked. Audrey, like most of the local women, always tried Ty first. If that didn't work, well then, she'd work her way down the pack hierarchy until she found a man who'd play along for the night. That was the way it worked. The women would try Cody next, and if they somehow struck out with him—hard to do, given Cody's willingness to please—then they would head for third choice.

Third choice came in two flavors. If the girls were after fresh meat with a strong dose of dark and tragic, they went to Kyle, the new guy on the ranch. If they wanted to prove how rebellious they could be, they came to Zack. He was the closest thing to the wrong side of the tracks the ranch had to offer, and the women found their way to him regularly.

Audrey's martyred sigh told him that she'd already exhausted options one and two.

"Cody is off with some other girl," she scowled.

Yeah, Zack figured as much.

"And Ty's off hunting for his phantom again," she grumbled. "The mate that doesn't exist."

Everyone knew that story: how Ty had fallen hard for an ephemeral scent that had come then simply disappeared. He'd hunted weeks for his destined mate, only to come back darker and emptier than before.

Audrey tugged Zack's elbow and pulled him around, bringing him face-to-face with her impossibly lush lips. "You know what they say about alphas."

That it was notoriously hard for strong characters to find their mates? Sure, Zack had heard that. And hell, maybe it was true. But at the moment, he was more concerned with warding Audrey off, now that she had her breasts crushed against his chest.

"You're an alpha inside, Zack." She came to the tips of her toes and let her moist lips brush his ear. "A big, strong man." Her hand ran south along his abs and teased at the top of his jeans. "Why don't you come out and find your mate?"

The woman was a siren, calling him toward a rocky shore. One he had no intention of wrecking on tonight, no matter what his animal wanted. It would be empty, meaningless—and he'd had plenty of that in his life. Just because women tried him out regularly didn't mean he took them all in. Especially Audrey. Especially tonight, with the scent of Rae—er, the full moon—still lingering around him like a smoky haze. He shouldn't have been able to scent anything over the barrage of odors coming from the cattle that morning, but Rae's distinct flavor had stayed front and center, finding its way past everything else to invade his senses.

And just like that, he jumped back in time to live it all again. The cattle, the fence, Rae. The bonfire she'd ignited in him.

"Zack, sugar?" Audrey called.

He blinked himself back to the present. The sun was low on the horizon, the sky starting to split into layers of red, orange, and yellow. He'd somehow made it through the work day and to this point. Quitting time, and time to head home. Alone.

"Gotta go," he mumbled, pulling away. "Find yourself another party, Audrey." Her face went from seductive to solid ice until he added his usual line. "You deserve better."

She flashed a satisfied smile and dropped a kiss on his cheek. "Don't sell yourself short, coyote."

He clenched his jaw. Right. He was just a coyote, but he shouldn't sell himself short. He suppressed a grimace as Audrey smoothed her skirt, reapplied her pouty look, and headed off into the night. To Kyle, no doubt.

He walked off, wishing his stride felt more purposeful and relaxed than it looked. It would be good to get some distance from his day. Good to get home to the cabin he'd grown up in. Like him, it stood on the fringes of pack society, firmly on ranch land but facing the coyote territory that bordered the ranch's western border. Funny how half of a man's blood could determine his whole being, at least as far as his wolf packmates were concerned.

He tried to blank his mind out. Just let it all go: the pack, his day, the subtle reminders of who he was and who he'd remain for the rest of his life. Third choice.

Usually, he could shed those thoughts like so many layers of clothing as he walked the rough path past acacia and graythorn. Tonight, though, that mechanism was off. Way off.

He sat a long time on his sloping porch, watching the stars blink on, one by one. The sight that normally brought him a sense of peace only mocked him tonight. And it only got worse when the moon rose over the horizon.

Aroooo...

A lazy howl sounded in the distance: one of the younger wolves, calling the pack out to play. Minutes later, the night came alive with voices. Some mournful, some teasing, others lusty. As usual, the full moon was bringing out the full range of emotion in wolves.

The longer he sat there, the harder it was to resist the moon's pull. He wanted to shift and run this itchy feeling off. Maybe Rae was out there. Maybe she'd let him lead her to a private spot. Maybe—

He shoved off his chair and headed inside. He'd call it an early night, that's what he'd do. He didn't understand why Rae was off-limits, but both Ty and old Tyrone had made it clear that she was not to be touched.

More like implied, his wolf complained.

Right, the coyote agreed. *They didn't actually forbid—*

He shoved them into the dog house he kept at the back corner of his mind and slammed the door on their protesting yelps.

It was no better, though, in bed, lying naked atop the sheets. Especially when the distant howls of his packmates grew more frenzied with the sounds of a lusty chase. Cody, by the sound of it, had found himself a willing playmate for the night. Barks turned to yowls of pleasure, male and female, that carried through the night.

Images flashed through Zack's mind, and the heat in his body rose. Images of Rae, tossing her ponytail behind her shoulder.

His hands slid from his ribs to his hips, down and up and back again.

He imagined Rae's gray eyes narrowing on him, swirling like harried clouds. Had she felt it, too?

He ran a palm over his groin, hastening the rush of blood, the hardening of flesh.

He pictured Rae's fingers playing over his shoulder, heating his skin as they went.

His fingers slid along the length of his cock, and his mind substituted her light touch for his, telling himself his wolf needed this.

He let his eyes slide shut and pretended it was her hand working him. She would glance up and those gray eyes would have darkened with desire. Her lips would part when her eyes dropped to his cock, and then she'd move down and take him with her mouth. Warm and wet and soft, it would be so much better than this crude self-service job of reality. Then she'd come up, looking dazed and lusty, and thrill him with the taste of himself on her lips. She'd lower her hips over his and take him in in one long, certain push. No hesitation, no games. Just two kindred souls united at last.

He dug his free hand into his own hip, making it hers, pulling her closer as he worked himself harder, faster. Going deeper and deeper as her eyes told him no man was his equal. None.

He continued until he was panting, then lying spent and shamefaced in the dark of his room, just as lost and lonely as the teenager he once was. What the hell was he doing?

He scowled out the open window. Whatever it was, he was definitely blaming it on the full moon.

Chapter Five

Rae was completely unaffected by her day. Completely unaffected by the full moon, too. And above all, completely unaffected by the man who'd invaded her senses before backing hurriedly away.

She knew this because she told herself so a hundred times throughout the day and into the night. Because being affected wasn't an option—not for a woman who knew exactly what she wanted.

Well, most of the time.

She lay on her bed, pillow pulled over her ears to block out the sounds of the night. It seemed that the wolves of Twin Moon Ranch reveled in the full moon like any other pack: they were loud, gleeful, and blissfully free of human inhibitions. Mated pairs sang sweet duets, howling their devotion into the night. The elders were hunched in a circle by the sound of it, voices joined with decades of practice as they sang an ode to generations past. Among them was a gritty bass that could only be the old alpha, joining in or warbling into silence whenever the hell he pleased. From farther out in the desert came the sound of the young and the restless, romping and yipping with the joy of youth, the thrill of desire.

That should be us out there, her wolf growled.

She ignored it. The last thing she needed was to go cavorting with a dozen randy males, all of them more than willing to initiate her into the pack in the most intimate way. A little bit of loose and easy didn't mean much, not with wolves, but some shifters had a way of letting too much carry over into the next day.

Not like I'd run with just anyone, the wolf sniffed. *Just with him. Zack.*

Rae pretended not to hear. *I just want to be left alone.*

So alone that we'll be alone forever?

She strained to pick his voice out from the others. Zack. A man she knew nothing about, except that his soul carried the scars of the past. A man whose power pulsed and glowed under the mantle of submission he pretended to wear. A man at home but not at home.

A man who flipped some dormant switch in her and set off a thousand blinking lights. Some soothed like Christmas bulbs strung on a tree, while others set off lightning bolts of anxiety.

A wolf needs its mate.

Enough with the mate nonsense, she snapped. *He's just another alpha-type. The same as the rest.*

This one is different, her wolf insisted.

How can you be sure? Alphas took what they wanted, when they wanted. Alphas were to be avoided at all costs.

He's not Jed.

He's worse, she retorted. *With ten times the power.*

And ten times the restraint. Couldn't you see it in him?

An image flashed in her memory: that moment right before Zack pulled away, his brow furrowed, eyes dark. The man wore a code of honor like a suit of armor. Restraint? Yes. But there was a reason for it. Under that armor was a powerful beast. What happened when it ran free?

He could set us free, her wolf whispered. *We want him. We need him.*

Outside, another wolf howl joined the rest, deep, gritty, and full of heartbreak. She froze, trying to place it. Not Zack, for all that she could picture him howling that way. But Zack's voice was smoother, more secretive. If anything, she'd guess that was Ty, standing apart from the others as he always seemed to do.

In the distance, another male sang in triumph, joined by a sultry female voice that purred satisfaction into the night. The moon urged; the body obeyed. It didn't have to mean more.

Except some men didn't get that. She hugged herself under the bedsheets. Some men thought that a female who was willing to put out as a wolf would be willing to hand her human body and soul over, too. Like Jed. One casual canine romp with him—the mistake of her life—and he thought he could claim her. He had her up against a wall the very next day, teeth bared at her neck, whispering all kinds of promises he'd never keep. He'd gone on about how happy she'd be serving him and how the two of them would someday rule their own pack.

Jed had gotten so carried away with his crazed vision, she thought he'd try to claim her that very night. All it would take was one deep bite in the right spot and she'd be bound to his whims and violent desires forever. Because a mating bite could be forced, and it was forever. The worst kind of forever.

She shook her head. If Jed was her destiny, she didn't want it.

Lucky for her, Greer—top dog of the Colorado pack—had come along and chased Jed away. Greer had saved her sorry little ass.

Unlucky for her, Greer had also taken notice of her sorry little ass, and something in his eyes said she hadn't won much of a reprieve from unwanted attention. Greer was a tyrant of an alpha who took what he wanted, when he wanted. Next to him, Roric of Nevada's Westend pack was a goddamn saint.

She drew the sheet over her head along with a long, deep breath, reminding herself of the long road she'd traveled since then. She'd fled her Colorado pack and started new in Nevada. From that point on, the only lovers she'd accepted were all low-ranking, easygoing types. And if sex with them left part of her unfulfilled, such was the price of protecting her soul.

Destiny is a myth, she told her wolf as gleeful howls carried through the night.

She flipped sideways in the bed, fighting the memories of Jed away. Her mother used to say, *to take away bad dreams, you need to bring in good ones.* So she tried conjuring up something safe and satisfying. Chocolate, maybe? It hardly fit the bill. The blanket she'd always slept under as a kid?

Slightly better. She tugged the imaginary fabric tight around her body, closed her eyes, and tried again.

Vague threads of color wove and combined into an image of a brown-haired, green-eyed stranger who carried the weight of the world on his shoulders, yet moved with silent grace.

Maybe Zack wasn't out cavorting with the others. Maybe he was at home in his cabin out by the mesa, where she'd seen him disappear to over lunch. What a perfect place that would be. A wisp of smoke in winter, the cooling shade of a sycamore in summer. It was just close enough to belong to the pack, but just far enough to call one's own.

Or maybe, her wolf cooed, *he's on his way over here right now.*

She tried pushing the thought away but found herself too weary to resist. If the vision insisted on intruding into her dreams, so be it. As long as it didn't happen in real life. Her imagination turned the tap of a tree branch into a soft knock at the door, and the fantasy took off.

"Rae."

He'd whisper from the doorway where he'd be standing, silhouetted by moonlight.

"Zack," she'd call softly and reach out her hand.

He'd slip into her room, pull up a corner of the sheet, and slide in beside her.

She curled her arms around her torso and let the hug of comfort turn into a different kind of embrace. Slowly, she stroked the length of her body, making her nipples harden. What would Zack's hands feel like, traveling that same path? How would he hold the weight of his body when he lay with her? Was he a tender lover or a demanding one?

The former, she decided. After all, it was her fantasy. He would murmur something sweet and low while one strong hand cupped her breast and the other stroked her hair. Then his thumb would start working her nipple, the way her own thumb did now, and her aching body would press against his, asking for more. Then his hand would wander lower, stirring warm, wet need in lazy circles that would have her biting back a moan. This man would know just where to touch her, and how.

He was doing it now, she decided, and in the darkness, she imagined their eyes locking as he lined up their bodies and slid home. Skin on skin, his heat would consume her. They'd move slowly at first then harder and faster until they hit a perfect rhythm. His movements would grow more urgent, his face tighter as they both climbed to the top of a mighty peak, then tumbled over the other side together.

They would come together again and again, first in the guesthouse she'd been assigned to, and then over in the cabin by the mesa. Her heart soared with every imagined encounter, every shuddering climax. When they ventured outside, she would let him press her up against the very fence where they'd first touched and bring her as high as the stars, as bright as the moon. Then they'd shift and run together into the desert, and the howls of joy would be their own.

Arooo....

Her fantasies carried her straight through the night and into the next morning, staying with her even after she rose, stretched, and headed to breakfast in the community dining hall. The sun was shining, the birds singing, and still the glow lingered.

She yawned. Too bad it was only her imagination that had experienced so many fantasies last night.

The dining hall door banged open, and a tall figure stepped out. Rae stopped dead in her tracks, facing her fantasy, this time in the flesh. When Zack's gaze caught hers, he stopped cold.

For a minute, all she registered was the hazel of his eyes and the thump of her heart. The whiff of unmasked lust reaching out to her like an arm. Then a voice behind her startled them both.

"Oh, Rae, Zack, have you met?" It was Tina, the alpha's daughter, who'd been the first person to welcome Rae to the ranch.

Heat filled Rae's cheeks as she forced a smile. "Yes, we have."

It might have been the morning light, but Zack's deep tan seemed to have a splash of red in it, too. His scent, however, had gone from full heat to guardedly neutral. The man was an enigma, impossible to read.

"Mmm." His deep hum reminded her of Nevada: the rare sound of distant thunder behind the clouds. "We have." He nearly left it at that, but then he rushed on. "Met, I mean."

"Yes, we have met," she echoed in a wobbly voice.

Most intimately, her wolf added with a satisfied yowl.

Chapter Six

Ten days. Zack had been counting. Ten days since the day Rae had pressed him into the fence, and damn it, he still couldn't let the feeling go. What started as a tingle turned to an itch and then a burning need that was spilling over from the fantasies of nighttime to the broad light of day.

Of course, his blame-it-on-the-moon theory was getting stretched thin, especially now that the full globe waned to a three-quarter silhouette and an ever-slimmer crescent, but he liked it better than the alternative.

What fool doesn't know his destined mate? his wolf growled. The beast had been clawing at his inner cage for days now.

Zack shoved the suggestion down every time.

Mate? Hell, no.

Destiny didn't work that way. Not for him, it didn't. Destiny was a bitter old spinster who showered rewards on a select few while pushing mudslides at everyone else. That was the way it was.

He told every part of his body and soul that, drilling the message into the furthest reaches of his mind. His duty was to the pack, and the pack—in the form of its second-in-command, Ty—wanted him to protect Rae. To keep the others away.

So he prowled, snarled, and hurled murderous looks at any male over the age of twelve who dared glance Rae's way. He'd guard her, all right.

In no time, he'd succeeded in creating a no-go zone around the newest member of the pack. Even Cody, who chased skirts the way a dog chased a ball, steered clear of Rae—almost suspiciously so. The best Zack could figure was that Rae must be some distant relative of the alpha's family. Why else would she be off-limits? Whatever the cause, he didn't care. The fewer men around his woman—he cleared his throat and corrected himself—*this* woman, the better.

Rae, meanwhile, seemed to go about her work unconcerned—unless Zack ventured too near. Then he sensed it again; the tremble of uncertainty, the hitch in her step. The same thing that happened to him if he got too close. So they tiptoed around each other, day after day.

She'd been sticking to herself, going about her work quietly and efficiently, taking meals apart from the others. Twin Moon pack didn't get many visitors, but those who did either settled in quickly or got the hell out. Rae hadn't done either—not yet. The woman consistently sought out the edge.

A little like him.

So it was no surprise to find her alone on the tenth evening, out in a little hollow at the foot of the hills where the desert smelled greener, the sage sweeter. The place where she had set up an impromptu archery range and practiced every evening. Twilight seemed to draw her there like a doe to a secret watering hole.

The only surprise was that his feet had brought him there, too. Didn't they get the memo about keeping away from her? Straying too close held danger, he knew. Next time, it might be him pressing into her. And if he started, God knows how he'd find the willpower to stop.

Thwack!

His ears flicked at the dull, striking sound. Rae was at it again. He'd never met a shifter who practiced archery, let alone a female shifter who did. But there she was, standing tall and lean, drawing back an arrow like one of Robin Hood's goddamn Merry Men transplanted to the desert. You'd have to have the eyes of a hawk to hit the distant target in this slanting light, but Rae nailed it every time.

She was all business: her hair pulled into a loose ponytail, long legs shoved into an earth-colored pair of overalls that couldn't hide the lithe curves of an athlete. Every inch of her screamed, *Expert! Stand back!* as if she knew something no one else knew. Like she could do things no one could even imagine.

There was something different about her, without a doubt. He just couldn't pinpoint what it was. It was more than just the trimmings: the bow, arrow, and wary attitude. There was something about the way her blue-gray eyes studied the sky, like she was waiting for some sign. A sign of what?

Thwack!

Another arrow, another perfect shot. He sidled a step closer. Watching from a distance would have been smarter, but his feet brought him right to the edge of the hollow.

Rae curved an arm up and over her shoulder, flipping the harvest gold ponytail aside to draw another arrow from the quiver strapped across her back. Her fingers tested the fletching the way a musician might test the strings of a guitar, and he couldn't help but imagine those fingers brushing over his back. The first one would be coarse and callused, scrubbing his skin. The second smoother, the third a tease, and the fourth finger—the pinkie—would be a butterfly on the heels of the rest. He imagined her doing that over and over, slowly coaxing the tight knots of his back into blissful release.

Thwack!

He took another step forward, coaxed on by a hypnotic inner voice. Not his wolf half this time, but the coyote: the clever, scheming half of his soul.

Just a little closer, it whispered. *Won't do any harm. Just one more step. Just a little—*

"Getting ready to kill someone?"

He heard the words before even realizing they were his own, murmured in her ear. Somehow, the last couple of steps had happened all on their own. And somehow, his voice was steady despite the blood hammering in his ears.

Rae tensed, though she casually brushed a lock of hair behind an ear as if she weren't surprised to find a near-stranger at her side.

"Depends," she muttered.

"Depends on what?"

"Depends how much *someone* pisses me off."

Okay, so he'd snuck up on her. Stealing up unnoticed was one of his best tricks. Coyotes knew stealth—one of the few things about that part of his ancestry that did him any good.

Rae was playing it cool, but his coyote caught the flare of her nostrils, the pink flush on her cheeks. Either she was annoyed at being caught off guard or she liked having him so close.

Maybe a little of both. His coyote grinned and decided to push a little more.

Never mind that he was supposed to be keeping guys away from her.

Of course not, his coyote huffed. *We're just doing our job. Keeping a close eye on her.*

Right. Not showing inappropriate interest. Not salivating over whatever it was about her that was so... so... irresistible.

Well, trying not to, anyway.

"And what does it take to piss you off?" the coyote made him say.

She kept her eyes firmly fixed on the target. "You don't want to find out."

Zip! The arrow's flight sounded different from up close, but the effect was the same: another shaft nestled amongst the dozen bristling from the bull's-eye. Part of him wouldn't have minded if that arrow had gone wide of its mark, giving away her emotions. But Rae was cool, calm, collected.

He hid a smile. He'd been worried about other men getting too close to her, but clearly, this woman was not someone to mess with. And yet she let him this close. Why?

"Calling it open season on straw targets?"

"Archery season on pronghorn opens next week," she murmured, lips against the string.

"You like to hunt?"

"I like to chase."

So do I, his wolf nodded, licking his lips.

For a moment, he wondered if she'd somehow caught that. Because her lips parted and her shoulder dipped just enough to make him wonder if she felt it, too. This link. This pull. Like the two of them were a couple of wobbly magnets suspended in that moment of truth before the poles finally made up their minds on whether they'd line up or repel.

"What's the bow for, if you're just going to chase?"

She fingered the barbed tip. "Just in case."

"In case of what?"

He watched Rae's eyes close on some ugly memory and regretted the question immediately. Wary fingers stroked the shaft like a talisman, and just like that, her easygoing veneer vanished, revealing something hard and angry beneath.

"In case I find the right kind of prey."

Zack sniffed and found the peppery scent of fear intertwined with the ammonia odor of hate. Or was that shame? His mood shifted in a heartbeat. Had Rae been mistreated by some shit of a man once upon a time? Had she been hurt?

His mind replayed what the ranch rumor mill had been saying about her. Where was she from — Nevada? Or was it Colorado? There was a pack up there rumored to have a brutal alpha. One who rode supreme over the minds and bodies of his pack. The kind who liked to break his pack in and ride them hard.

Literally.

The kind of alpha who would snuff out a soul just to show he could.

He could picture why an alpha would be drawn to a woman like Rae. She had that inner spark, that flame. A woman who could bring out the best—or the worst—in a wolf. But Rae was too restless and independent to ever settle for being an alpha's mate.

He didn't even realize she'd released the next arrow until he heard the furious smack of it. Bull's-eye.

In one smooth move, she pulled another arrow from her quiver, notched it, and took aim. The woman was a wall of ice, her gray eyes thunderous as they narrowed on the target.

Zip! The arrow flew, sending a clear message. *I am not a woman to fuck with. I will chase the past away.*

Zack shifted his weight back, even as the coyote inside ran his tongue over his lips. The more she pushed him away, the more he wanted her.

The *coyote* wanted her, he told himself. Only the coyote. The man knew where to draw the line.

But there was a wolf in there, too. And Rae was so irresistibly untamed. Wild and free, unfettered by the expectations of society.

At the moment, though, she was tenser than her recurve bow. Time to ease off.

"You got a hunting tag for that pronghorn, miss?" he teased, dropping his voice in his best sheriff's imitation.

"Don't need one," she huffed, feigning annoyance though her voice was laced with relief. He'd hit the right tone, at last. "Not for the kind of hunting I do."

His pulse jumped, wondering what kind of hunting that was.

"And wolf?" he ventured. "Got a tag for that?" God, when had he become so... so forward?

Rae gave an exaggerated sigh. "You haven't figured out yet that I'm not interested?"

That's what she said, but everything about her screamed the opposite. The catch in her voice, the sharp intake of each breath, the sweet scent of arousal enveloping her like perfume.

"I think you are," his coyote made him whisper, much too close to her ear.

She let out an exasperated huff, like he'd been hounding her for a week instead of a minute. Why he was doing it, he didn't know. Only that the coyote was to blame. Oh, and the moon, too, no matter what phase it was in.

"I figure a guy like you must have plenty of women to mess around with."

That barb went right to his gut. "Think I'm messing around?"

"You're missing the point," she murmured out of the side of her mouth, sending his eyes down the arrow's shaft until they found the steel tip. "I don't mess around." On that, she sealed her lips, took aim, and released.

Thwack!

Zack didn't have to look to know it was another perfect shot.

"Neither do I," he insisted, though he knew he should back off. But it was true: he wasn't messing around. This was sheer need. Instinct. Whatever it might be called, he couldn't fight it away. And suddenly, he didn't want to any more.

So when her eyes fell to his lips and lingered there long enough for him to be sure, he acted on impulse. The next thing he knew, his hand was on her shoulder and his lips reaching for hers. When they connected, the surprise in her eyes was replaced by something soft, willing, and lonely enough for him not to break away. A look like the one he sometimes found in the mirror, the few times he bothered to check.

A heartbeat later, his eyes locked away the world, focusing entirely on the kiss. Rae's lips were sweet and soft and tangy, a secret elixir brewed just to stir his soul. That was what a hummingbird must feel when it closed in on nectar: a world bursting with color, texture, flavor. And the taste of her! Sweet and shy and unexpected, like wild blackberries that only cropped up in good years. The ones you were lucky to get a handful of before they'd gone, quick as they'd come.

Rae's scent was like all of spring concentrated into a single day, a single moment. His lips moved with unspoken words, while hers curved and bent in echo. Rae leaned into him, her lithe frame fitting perfectly alongside his.

Perfect. Home. Mine. Thoughts bounced like tumbleweeds through the uneven landscape of his mind.

The bow went limp at her side and her hand slid around his ribs, tugging him closer. Zack had the vague feeling he might be running out of air.

"Rae," he whispered, and even those three letters tasted sweet.

Her eyes flicked open, the gray warm and soft as a fair weather cloud at sunrise.

But the very next instant, she tensed. Her eyes jumped, and she pulled away. His wolf let out a whine, wanting to explain that he would never hurt her. He would hold her, love her, protect her. Forever.

But Rae was scuttling backward, her face on the rise behind them. Someone was coming.

Zack swung quickly to the woodpile while she pulled another arrow and faced the target as if nothing had happened. The two of them were perfect conspirators already, though they'd shared nothing more than a kiss.

A twig snapped and a voice cursed, breaking the peace of the hollow. Zack spun around, every muscle primed to defend his mate.

"You," came a curt, accusing call.

Zack's spine stiffened as Tyrone stepped into view. What the hell was the old man doing out here?

The alpha approached, power radiating off him like a living, breathing thing.

"You."

He stuck an accusing finger at Rae, and Zack immediately stepped into the man's path. Alpha or no alpha, no man was coming near Rae.

Tyrone shot him a look that was pure malice then turned his sights to Rae. "You shouldn't be here alone."

She's not alone, Zack wanted to point out. *She's got me.*

The old alpha reached out, fingers aimed for their usual spot on the back of his neck. Every time the alpha did it, Zack let him. He had to; it was the way of the pack.

But this time, the coyote dug in its hind feet and refused to be swayed. Whether the beast was trying to impress Rae or just plain crazy, he couldn't tell. Only that he'd had enough. Taking a tiny side step, he let the alpha's hand land on his shoulder, short of its mark. Tyrone's eyes widened and flashed.

Test me, old man, Zack's coyote nearly said. *Try it.*

The alpha's eyes flicked from Zack to Rae and back again, lips curling down.

"Time to do what you do best, boy," Tyrone spat, turning every word into an insult. He pulled Zack aside, fingernails biting into his flesh. *And if I find you anywhere near this woman again,* his glare added, *I'll skin your no-good coyote alive.*

Before Zack could compose a reply, the old man went on. "We've gotten word of a possible trespasser."

At that, the old man gave Zack a shove toward the ranch. And in the old days, Zack might have stumbled along on command. Now, he took a single, stiff step—the shortest possible movement that wouldn't ignite a battle. He didn't need one, not with an inner battle already raging over Rae. The effect she had on him. The reaction his inner wolf and coyote—in agreement, for a change—both had to her.

Mine. Mate!

The words flicked like fireflies through his mind. Much as he wanted to watch them glow and play, he knew he had to snuff them out. It couldn't be. There was no mate for him, no peace. Just a trespasser to track. That was his duty; the ruling alpha said so.

Duty, his wolf nodded.

Mate, the coyote cried.

Tyrone broke the impasse with a second, angry shove. "Go! Get on it. You understand me, boy?"

Oh, he got it all right. When the old man said *trespasser*, he meant the shapeshifter kind. The kind looking for trouble. Straying onto pack territory without permission was more than an insult: it was a crime. And a danger to his pack was a danger to Rae. Any trespasser who intruded on pack territory—and into this crazy *something* between him and Rae—was dead meat.

Rae's gray eyes found his and hung on for all they were worth. Her face was hard, but her gaze softened just enough to make his ribs tighten.

Duty? Mate?

Zack tore himself away. If he kept thinking along those lines, he'd be the one who was dead meat.

Chapter Seven

Two days passed in which Rae told herself the ranch didn't feel any different with Zack gone, but it was impossible to kid herself. Something was missing, even if it was just his unmistakable presence. The man was like a mesa after dark: a brooding, lonely mass caught somewhere between the past and the future.

It doesn't have to be that way, her wolf said. *He can have better. He can have us.*

Look who sounds all haughty, she shot back. *Not like I'm such a prize.*

Ah, but I am, the wolf purred.

That part, at least, was true, and she nearly smiled at her secret.

Another part was true, too: Zack could do better than playing second fiddle to the alpha-in-waiting. A healthy pack needed more than a single leader, and Ty seemed man enough to recognize that. The problem, as far as she saw it, was that Ty and Zack were still the boys they'd once been, subservient to the old alpha. What would it take to shake up the old guard?

On the other hand, was it any of her business? No. For all she knew, Zack didn't want better. Maybe he didn't even know what better was.

We can show him, her wolf said, glowing at the memory of his kiss. A kiss that had been a gamble, a hope, and a promise, all wrapped together. Electrifying and soothing, assuring her there was a place on this Earth for her: a happy, safe, and serene place close to him.

She gave herself an inner shake. A kiss could be a brand, too, marking her as his. That was the danger: an alpha male deciding she belonged to him. She'd already fled that threat twice. She didn't want to be anybody's. She wanted—needed—to be her own.

So she did her best to pretend she didn't miss Zack and concentrated on doing her job without drawing attention to herself. That was the key, especially now that the new moon was sneaking up.

She worked her way down the fence line on the southwest side of the ranch, checking every beam. The midday sun sucked all the life out of the air, and heat pressed down over the landscape like a sheet of lead. The buzz of honest activity that had so captivated her when she'd first arrived on the ranch seemed lackluster today.

Funny the difference one lonely tracker could make.

That much about Zack, she'd gathered. He was a tracker, and not just any tracker, but the best in the Four Corners region. She'd learned as much from the sweet old woman everyone called Aunt Jean. Jean seemed to be the unofficial matron of the pack, given that the grizzled old alpha had never taken a mate.

"If it's on two feet, our Zack can find it," old Jean had said with pride.

Rae's wolf ears perked at that. *What about tracking something on four feet?*

If her tail had been out, she'd have given it a lusty swipe.

She slapped a firm hand over her thigh, warning the beast to cool it. But even that couldn't keep her from imagining a nocturnal chase. She, the quarry, he, the tracker. Now that would be a fun game.

Hunting isn't a game, she reminded herself, hearing the echo of her grandmother's words, spoken long ago in what seemed a different lifetime, a different place.

Love isn't a game, either, her wolf replied.

In the distance, the lunch bell sounded, calling the ranch hands to the dining hall, but Rae kept working. Coming in at the tail end of a meal meant less time making polite small talk. Not that she didn't like the others; it was just that the company she wanted wasn't there today.

She bent down to test the lower beam of the fence, and that's when she heard it: a step behind her, then another.

When she whirled, the approaching figure—all six-plus feet of him—threw his hands up like a guilty man expecting an accusation.

She cocked her head. It was Ty, the alpha's son and heir apparent. She'd only ever seen him from a distance—and always, always exuding that nuclear-power aura that kept everyone at arm's length. But right now, his eyes were on the ground, his demeanor hesitant.

"Hi," he murmured, so low Rae could barely hear.

Her heart beat a little faster in the urge to flee.

"Hi," she forced herself to say. It came out clipped and hurried. Cold.

Ty glanced back toward the ranch, and for a second Rae thought she saw the imposing figure of his father scowling from the shadows. But noon in the desert had a way of playing tricks on the eyes; it was probably just in her head.

Ty stuck his hands in his pockets and kicked at the ground as if maybe he could find a cue card among the pebbles and dirt.

"How you doing?" he asked after a long, quiet minute had passed. "I mean, how are you settling in?" His gaze was reluctant, the corners of his dark eyes sad.

That was the only thing that kept Rae from sprinting off. Ty wasn't there to harm or demand. He was there to...to... Wait. Why had the second-highest ranked wolf in the pack gone out of his way to talk to her, looking at her like she was a problem he couldn't solve?

"Um...fine."

In truth, she was more than fine. Arizona suited her perfectly, and her heart sang with every whisper of the clean, dry wind. There was nothing she missed about Westend pack, and nothing she could fault in the way Twin Moon pack worked in quiet harmony with the earth.

But she'd be even more fine if Ty left her alone—and finer still if Zack were around. The tracker had a way of either soothing her pulse or making it thump in excitement. Ty, on the other hand, set off all her alarms. Who he was and what he represented scared her. He was a man of power, and power had a way of corrupting men—even good men.

"Good." Ty nodded, but his tone was unenthusiastic, as if he might have preferred a different answer.

"Good," she echoed.

God, this was awkward. What did he want? She looked south, avoiding his eyes, and he looked north, avoiding hers.

"You coming to lunch?" he finally asked.

She couldn't quite say no, but she didn't want to say yes. "Soon."

He nodded and stared into the distance with the hollow gaze of a man who'd given up on wishes and hopes. So much, she almost ached for him. Even with everything she'd had to escape in her past—two brutes in Colorado and a suffocating pack in Nevada—she'd never given up hope. Hope to find a place she could call home. A place like this, maybe.#

If only everyone would just leave her alone.

Ty might have read her mind, because he gave her a grim nod and strode away. Quickly.

She watched him go, wishing it was Zack coming and not a man she had no interest in going. But at least Ty was giving her some space, and she was happy for that.

She checked another three sections of fence before pocketing her hammer and heading back to the heart of the ranch. What had that strange encounter been all about?

She loitered every step of the way, watching a bird sip from the irrigation ditch, then flit into the shade of a palo verde tree. Her feet took her on a long detour to the ranch gate, as they'd done nearly every day. Something about the way the proud, simple structure framed the landscape fascinated her. The solid trunks of two ponderosa pines formed the sides, supporting a long cross-beam high overhead. At the midpoint hung the ranch brand: two circles, overlapping by a third.

Twin Moon Ranch. The name fit the place perfectly.

She stepped to the threshold of the gate then paused. One step farther and she'd be in the outside world. One step back and she would be firmly on the ranch. She rocked on the balls of her feet, undecided. Was the ranch a prison or a sanctuary? Which way to go?

Forward, she coached herself. *Out.* That was the way to go. To find her freedom and her destiny, whatever it might be.

Her wolf sniffed. *Or free to stumble into the biggest mistake of your life. Your choice. Our destiny could be right here.*

She wavered, and then took a step back, wondering what held her in place.

We're waiting, silly, her wolf said.

Waiting for what?

For Zack to return.

Rae wanted to snort. *That's pathetic.*

It's romantic, the wolf insisted.

If it's so romantic, why did he leave?

The wolf just shrugged. *Duty.*

Ah, the simplicity of a wolf's mind.

A wolf might be content with that kind of life—waiting at home like a good little mate—but not a woman who could stand on her own two feet.

Well, Zack's not here, and now we have Ty sniffing around. That's the last thing we need.

The wolf gave a lazy huff. *He wasn't sniffing. He wasn't interested. Not a whiff of lust on him.*

"Thank God." Rae said that part out loud. But what did he want?

Not us, her wolf shrugged.

Rae had to give the wolf that. Whatever Ty wanted, it wasn't her, and she was happy for that. Let the other women heave longing looks him at that mountain of a man. She wasn't interested. Not in him, at least.

She glanced at the sky, where a hawk soared in broad circles. There was something magical about watching a fellow hunter at work: wheeling, gliding, choosing exactly the right instant to swoop in toward its prey. She knew what the casual lift of its feathertips meant: today was just another day of many, but tonight... Tonight was the night of the new moon.

Even her wolf couldn't hold back a shiver of anticipation, knowing what that meant. The blackest, deepest night, a night when time stood still but for the slow arc of stars overhead.

A new moon called to her the way a full moon called to the others. Every wolf in every pack had a duty, but Rae—she had a higher calling, one that superseded duty to any one pack.

Tonight, she promised herself. She'd put Zack, Ty, and everyone else out of her mind and remind herself who she was and what she had to do.

To do that, though, she needed more space, because roaming too close to the others might expose what she was. A glance at the sun, swinging past its zenith, said she'd better get moving soon. She would have to drive a couple of hours north then set out on foot to find what she sought.

So she headed to the dining hall, gobbled down a quick meal, and jotted a note to leave on the guesthouse bed. She ought to ask the alpha's permission before leaving the ranch, but technically, she was headed to a distant corner of the vast property, so that didn't quite apply.

Be back soon, the note said.

Soon? Her wolf laughed.

Well, *soon* sounded more polite than *Whenever I damn well please.* She stared at the paper, wishing she could write exactly that. Would she ever find a pack that understood what destiny had intended for her?

She waited until the others had all settled back into work then grabbed her bow and arrows and headed for the battered old Ford she'd driven over from Nevada. She'd scrimped for months to buy it just for the sake of independence and pride. For convenience, too, and the security of an escape pod, should the need arise.

The thrill of car ownership was still there as she hopped in and took off. Driving out the gate was easy once she'd picked up a little mental momentum. She drove three miles down the dirt road, made a sharp left onto the highway, and headed north, where the pull in her bones pointed.

North. That's where she would find her prey.

Chapter Eight

It started well, as every promising hunt should.

Rae drove a couple of hours north and then out on a long, winding side road, letting instinct guide her to her prey. But then the engine started laboring and spouting steam before finally rattling to a stop.

She got out, popped the hood, and studied the smoking engine long enough to conclude she had no idea what to do.

Crap.

She lifted her head and looked around. Closing her eyes, she sniffed and found a whiff of hope. A broken-down car she could deal with—later. The important thing was, she was close enough to continue on foot. She could sense her quarry out there, not far away. Soon it would be dark, and the hunt would be on.

The hunt. Her lips curled into a smile.

Anvil-shaped clouds rumbled along the horizon like an enemy army in full march, but that hardly mattered. Her quarry's scent was strong and vibrant. Of course, finding her prey was rarely an issue. The trick was catching it.

It was still daylight, though; a little too early to close in on her prey. She pulled a water bottle from the back seat and drank her fill. Let the sun set. Let the clouds thunder in. Let the car wait. She would be like the hawk wheeling in the sky, biding its time.

She lifted the bottle to her lips, but stopped abruptly and turned. A plume of dust rose from the dirt road, coming her way. The back of her neck prickled in alarm when she caught sight of a dark red pickup with tinted windows. Every muscle in her body went stiff.

Trouble. Trouble for sure.

She pulled her bow out from the open window of the back seat along with a silver-tipped arrow—just in case. Then she spun back to the road, notching the arrow just as the truck came to a halt and the front door creaked open.

Her fingers stroked the fletching as she waited, prepared to fend off the stranger if necessary. She had several weapons to choose from: words, fangs, or the tip of her arrow. She'd start with one and move on to the others as the situation called for.

It was only when her nose got hold of his scent that she trembled inside. Behind the scent of tobacco, stale beer, and a cheap cologne was the unmistakable peaty musk of a shifter. A wolf shifter, one of her own kind.

A big brute of a man unfolded himself from the car.

"Hello, Sunshine." He grinned. "It's been a long time."

Rae froze. It had been years since anyone used that stupid nickname. Her eyes flicked to the car and found the green and white ridgeline of Colorado plates. When they jumped back to the stranger's face, everything clicked into place.

A cocky man driving a truck with Colorado plates. One with a cleft chin so deep, you could hide a dime in it. One who called her a name she hadn't heard in years.

A nightmare straight out of her past.

"So happy to see me, you're speechless?" he chuckled.

"Jed." She nodded, forcing all emotion out of her voice.

It really was him. Or more like an extra-large version of the old Jed. He'd always been big and cocky, and she'd always known he'd grow into a force to be reckoned with. But this? The teenager who'd been growing like a weed had bulked up and added eighty pounds of muscle. His chiseled face was accented by a sharp line of facial hair that followed his jaw from ear to either side of that cleft chin. He stroked it as he looked her up and down, his gaze slow, sure, and hungry.

"Little Sunshine, all grown up," Jed murmured. Then his eyes narrowed and he launched right into conversation as if they'd left off ten minutes ago instead of ten years. "I meant what I said, Sunshine. You and me got great things ahead of us."

He was just as crazy as he'd been back then. Crazier, even. Rae stepped back and held the bow higher, keeping the arrow notched.

"How did you find me?"

He grinned like the devil on a hot, sultry night. "Got a nose for my mate, Sunshine."

"I'm. Not. Your. Mate." She broke the words up, so that maybe this time, they would penetrate that thick head.

He only grinned wider, flashing the points of his canines. "You always did like to play."

She eyed the empty landscape for some avenue of escape. Jed's version of play most likely meant violent sex followed by a mating bite that would bond her to him forever. No way. She ordered her racing heart to calm down, her freewheeling mind to think.

Last she had heard, the alpha of North Ridge pack in Colorado was still Greer Roberts. And last she'd heard, he was still a ruthless tyrant. Had he sent Jed to track her? Unlikely. Jed would have been cast out a few years ago, before he stirred up too much trouble. Less stable packs did that with powerful up-and-comers, lest they challenge the leadership. The young bucks roamed restlessly, causing trouble until they found a place they liked the look of and staged a takeover, challenging the local alpha in a fight to the death.

"You and me, we'll head back home." Jed outlined his plan in a tone more suited to weekend plans than a major power play. "I take out Greer, we rule the pack. What?" He paused, seeing her jaw go slack. "Greer's a self-centered, greedy ass who has no business being alpha."

So are you, she nearly pointed out. Did Jed really think he could take on Greer, the biggest, baddest alpha she'd ever seen?

But this new version of Jed was pretty damn big and bad. Maybe, just maybe, youth would triumph over experience. Not that North Ridge pack would benefit either way.

"I'm never going back," she insisted, scanning the area. Using her bow at close range was a fifty-fifty proposition, but if she shifted into her wolf form, she could outrun Jed. The question was, had he come alone?

"Sure you will." He nodded, all smiles but for the warning in his eyes.

A second engine sounded in the distance, and her gut sank.

"Friend of yours?" Jed growled, turning to the source.

A sleek black motorcycle came roaring down the road, kicking up a trail of dust that reached toward the ever-darker sky.

Right. She wished. A friend with a fast bike and a perfect sense of timing would come in awfully handy right now. A friend with an old-fashioned black helmet and biceps that bulged as he roared up and squealed to a stop. A friend with a fierce countenance who would jump off the bike and toss his helmet aside.

"Who is this asshole?" Jed jabbed a thumb in the newcomer's direction.

Rae blinked. "Zack?"

It really was him, though his whole bearing had changed. He was taller, darker, meaner. For a moment, he looked more like a man who could shift into a fire-breathing dragon instead of a wolf.

"Who is *this* asshole?" Zack growled back.

Chapter Nine

Zack looked the intruder up and down, slowly taking him in. Then he glanced at Rae. Did she know this ass?

Step by wary step, he and the intruder circled each other, two paces apart.

"You're looking at the future alpha of North Ridge pack," the ass had the nerve to say with a perfectly straight face.

Cocky son of a bitch. Zack sniffed and got a lungful of raw wolf power. But it was all bulk and bluster, no brains or balls.

"Give it a break, Jed," Rae muttered, crossing her arms over her chest.

Jed? Zack's wolf bristled. *Who the hell is Jed?*

A good thing he had arrived in time, before... before... Well, he didn't want to imagine what this ass wanted with Rae. Only that it wasn't good, and she didn't want any part of it. That much was crystal clear.

His pulse spiked just from seeing her again. It had only been a couple of days, but the ache for her had only gotten worse. He'd been rushing through his tracking job as fast as he could.

Normally, it was the opposite with him: he loved the feeling of being out in the desert alone. But this time, something felt off. The minute he'd left the ranch, he'd been haunted by the feeling that he'd forgotten something in that timeworn shack he called home.

Something. Maybe even someone.

Zack had told himself it wasn't her, but the minute he did, his wolf got all worked up again, pulling him away from duty and back to her. So he'd tracked long and hard to hurry up and get the job done. So far, he'd tracked and rid the property of three intruders. Two had the good sense to run off, while the third was stupid enough to think that he might best an angry werewolf on his home turf.

That one was dead.

He'd had a fourth in his sights when the call came. Rae had been reported missing on the ranch, and old Tyrone was throwing a fit.

"She's run off," the old alpha snarled into the phone. "Track her. Find her. Bring her back."

Zack didn't like the alpha's urgency. Audrey had once taken off for three weeks when she'd hooked up with a passing trucker and no one had blinked an eye. Why the three-bell alarm when Rae had only been gone for a few hours? Why did she merit the special attention?

Was she the daughter of another alpha, maybe? She didn't seem like the type. Too flighty. Too defensive. Too damn modest.

He just didn't get it. But he'd done as he was told and dropped everything to track her—which was easy, as it turned out. She'd been in his general area, and it wasn't like he could miss her scent once he was tuned in to it. He'd picked it up from miles away; there was something regal and Old World in it. Then it was just a case of racing after her. That was one of the advantages of his Harley—the one useful thing his father had ever left him, even if it had been half-wrecked at the time.

The crazy thing was, he'd not only found Rae, but another trespasser, too. This jerk, Jed.

"Future alpha, huh?" Zack asked, unimpressed.

Jed puffed his chest out another inch. "Got that right."

If it were just him and the intruder, Zack would have launched straight into a fight, even if he knew it meant risking death. Jed might not know much, but he obviously knew how to fight. Big, young, and cocky added up to danger in its own way, and Jed had the brash confidence of a young gun who'd yet to be put in his place.

Zack would have been happy to do just that, even if meant the fight of his life. But Rae was standing right beside him, and prudence held him back from launching into flesh-tearing violence. Right now, it was better to keep his cool and go for the diplomatic solution.

He could always kill the motherfucker later.

The prospect was tempting, given the way the ass was crowding Rae. Like he owned her. Like she was his.

Zack's wolf growled. *Mine!*

He superimposed an even tone over the low rumble in his chest. "Well, future alpha of North Ridge pack, you're trespassing on Twin Moon territory."

Jed threw his head back and laughed. "This ain't pack territory."

Zack lifted an eyebrow. "You sure about that?"

Jed's cool gaze lost its edge. Definitely not the brightest bulb. They were on ranch property, but the far outer fringes. There was no one here to contest Jed's intrusion but Zack. Not that he was going to tell Jed that.

"Of course, we can fight here and now to solve this," Zack started.

"We will," Jed growled and stepped closer. "And I will wipe your sorry ass straight into the dust."

Try me, his wolf snarled.

"Right," he said calmly. "Let's say you do. Then the whole pack will be on your ass, and the lady here will be less than impressed."

Jed's eyes slid to Rae, and for a moment Zack saw something like affection there. The question was whether the affection was for the woman or a lunatic's cocky vision of the future. Either way, he wanted those eyes off Rae and on him.

You touch her, I kill you. He hurled the words out, straight from his mind to Jed's.

Let Jed know exactly who he was dealing with. Let him show a little respect. That's what it always came down to. Respect.

He knew he had it when Jed's chin whipped over to him, eyes registering surprise. Bull's-eye. Now he really had the man off-balance, because few shifters could reach into the mind of a complete stranger.

Maybe we should try that trick with Tyrone someday, his coyote snickered.

Zack ignored him. It was time to get Rae out of Dodge. Keeping a firm eye on Jed, Zack tilted his head just enough for Rae to get the message. *Get on the bike.* His mind was already calculating—he could get her back to the ranch within a couple of hours, then turn around and chase Jed down.

He threw a leg over the bike and nodded Rae onto the back. The crazy woman detoured to grab her quiver of arrows out of the car first, which had him steaming, but once she slipped into place behind him, his innards went all warm at the barrage of sensations. Her thighs, clamped around his hips. Her breath, tickling his ear. The soft flesh of her breasts, pressing against his back. And most of all, that scent, like a whole season was clinging to her shoulders, ready for a wild ride.

Thunder clapped in the distance, snapping him out of his trance. The storm was close. Very close. He started the engine with a sharp kick and took off. Originally, he'd been thinking to head back to the highway, but the hills were a better place to take shelter, and he knew just the place to go.

His wolf hummed in recognition. *The cozy little cabin tucked in behind Scarecrow Mesa?*

Yes, that would be just the place.

Chapter Ten

They reached the cabin just after sunset and only seconds before the rain hit. Rae ran straight inside, holding the door for Zack. He pushed his Harley under the overhang of the porch then whisked right up to her, and they stood side by side, watching the storm break.

She'd never seen anything like it, not in Nevada, not in Colorado. The front edge of the clouds rolled and twisted, while dark, thin tendrils reached ahead of the mass like scouts. The storm was menacing. Powerful. Thrilling, too.

Only part of her attention was on the storm, though. The rest was on Zack, standing shoulder to shoulder with her while the thunder rumbled. His chest rose and fell as if he wanted to fight this intruder, too.

She breathed him in as if she hadn't been doing that for the past hour, half an inch away from his neck while the motorcycle throbbed between her knees. At first, she'd inhaled Zack's scent to settle her fears, because Jed was back after all this time. A crazy man on a mission—and he wanted her in on it. She'd been so absorbed in thinking ahead to her hunt that she let Jed sneak right up—her worst nightmare come true.

So she'd nestled deeper between Zack's broad shoulder blades and inhaled the thick scent of his leather jacket. She'd concentrated on the tiny curl of saddle-brown hair behind his ears and his steady heartbeat. Bit by bit, her anxiety faded, replaced by another emotion aroused by the heat of his body and the pulse of the engine.

Desire.

At least her nose had had the good grace to maintain a tiny distance because what her arms and legs had been up to under the guise of hanging on was positively scandalous. His heat pulled her in, inviting her hands to slip into his jacket pockets and trace everything underneath. Like the thick layers of muscle stretched diagonally over his ribs. Like the mogul course of his abdomen. Like the waistband of his jeans...

Thunder shattered the air, and Rae fought the urge to flinch.

"After you." Zack tilted his head toward the cabin doorway.

"After you." She echoed his movement, trying to keep her cool.

Zack arched one perfect eyebrow, and she held her breath. This was it. Either the alpha in him would show his true colors, or he would prove himself able to give and take.

The air around them crackled as the next stroke of lightning gathered its energy. She could feel the power building, building, waiting to snap.

Finally, after an endless stalemate, one corner of Zack's mouth twitched, and he headed in.

Rae exhaled, long and shaky, then followed. A lightning clap exploded, chasing her over the threshold and directly up to his chest.

Zack looked at her, wondering, perhaps, what demands she'd place on him next. There was only so far an alpha wolf could be pushed. So she took a step back and nodded at the rafters, pretending she hadn't noticed the king-size bed that took up most of the tidy space.

"Nice place."

He smiled a small, secret smile, the first she'd ever seen on her dark knight. If she hadn't been steeling herself to resist at all costs, that smile would have been devastating. A curl of those perfect lips, a crinkle in the corner of his eye, and the briefest flash of white teeth. Part of her heart melted right there, wondering what this man would look like if he had a little more joy in his life.

She forced away a lump in her throat. What would it feel like to be the one to help him find joy—not just in tiny doses on stormy nights but in broad daylight, too?

"The pack has a few cabins scattered around. Just in case," Zack said, nodding around the cozy space.

Rae leaned her bow in a corner, making sure to place the quiver at exactly the right angle for quick action.

Just in case, the stubbornest part of her insisted—the same part that said men were not to be trusted. She'd had a prime example of that not an hour ago with Jed. So what was she doing letting her guard down with Zack?

Lightning illuminated the single room in three distinct flashes, chased by a mighty clap of thunder. The storm was directly over them now, surging with power.

"How did you know where I was, anyway?" she asked.

Zack shrugged, as if finding her in a several hundred square miles had been child's play. "I'm a tracker. I track."

Anything on two feet, she remembered Aunt Jean saying.

"Wait. Why were you after me, anyway?"

As soon as she said it, she wanted to rephrase the sentence so he wouldn't take *after me* too literally. But Zack was already breaking into a mischievous grin.

She hid a smile. Maybe she should get him off the ranch more often. He seemed freer here, more at peace.

She leaned in, wanting more of that look, then froze at what she found. Deep in his eyes lurked a wolf, and the green of his irises shone with resolve.

I would come for you, the wolf said, *through a thousand fiery hells.*

That look went on for an eternity, and she wondered if she'd ever break free. She wondered if she even wanted to. Everything about Zack was honest, sincere, and strong—a promise that wrapped around her like a high, defensive wall. But when thunder clapped again, Zack blinked the look away. Mumbling something to himself, he pulled a phone from his pocket.

He dialed, held it up to his ear, and studied her. "What were you thinking, coming out here on your own?"

She opened her mouth, thought a second, then closed it. How much to tell him? How much to trust?

He lowered the phone and studied the display. "Shit." He squinted at her, like she'd hexed it or something. "No reception." His eyes bored deeper. "Why did you run away from the ranch?"

She huffed. "Can't a woman decide to hunt for a day or two without being accused of running away?"

"Hunt?" The way his eyes gleamed, she was sure his wolf liked the sound of the word.

A second ticked by, then another.

"You shouldn't be out here alone." He stepped so close, she had to tilt her head back to keep her eyes locked on his. The heat of him embraced her, pulling her even closer.

I'm not alone. Not any more, she wanted to say.

"You sound like someone I know," she said, testing him.

Zack fixed her with a deep, dark look that said her comment had cut deep. "I will never be like him," he said, punctuating each syllable.

Every sentence the man uttered was an oath: that he'd never be like Tyrone, the overbearing alpha, nor Jed, who took without asking, nor any other alpha she'd ever known. He was Zack, no more, no less.

"I know," she whispered, bowing her head so low, it touched her chest. But he was already shunning her, turning to the window to study the emptiness outside.

The emptiness inside, something whispered from the depths of her mind. That's what he was seeing.

Her wolf cursed. *Why do you keep pushing him away?*

Because a man can steal my freedom, croaked a voice from deep within her scarred memories.

This man can give us freedom, her wolf snarled back. *And we can give him his.*

At that moment, it felt as though they were both out in the open, being buffeted by the storm. The cabin stood in the eye of one of those electrifying desert storms that filled the sky with raw power without the relief of rain. Clouds were swirling, building, and heaving all around, kneading her emotions.

Trust. That was the issue. Was she capable of it, even for just one night? Zack had come after her. Not to drag her away, as Jed would have, but to protect her. What was the malice in that?

Lightning lit his downcast face. Thunder clapped right on its heels, nearly on top of them, but Zack didn't flinch, not even as the walls shook with the power of the storm.

Some spark of lightning must have leaped over to Rae, because her lips tingled the way they had when Zack had kissed her. The feeling raced along her synapses, igniting something in her soul.

Maybe it didn't have to be one or the other: her freedom or a man. Maybe for once, she could give herself the freedom to take a man—a real man, an alpha. Like Zack, who promised her everything while asking for nothing.

Her wolf gave a long, lusty *grrrr*.

Tomorrow, she reasoned, she would have plenty of time to be alone. Her whole life had been spent alone. So why not give herself this one night, far from the reach of the pack?

One short step and she was at his side, a hand resting on his waist. Layers of muscle, one chiseled over another, bundled around his torso like overlapping sheets of armor. She wanted to feel his arms around her the way she'd had hers around him on the motorcycle.

Trust. She pulled it around her like a blanket and then tugged the edge over toward him. With one quick inhale, she was on her toes, reaching for his brow with her fingers. No, with her lips. Because she wanted more than a stolen kiss. She wanted more of this man.

All of him, if only for one night.

Chapter Eleven

Zack had given up counting the beats between sledgehammer blows of thunder and flashes of lightning. They were right on top of each other now, cracking directly overhead.

If only his brain could catch up to his body the same way. Because the more Rae melted into him, the harder he grew. His shoulders pulled back, his stomach knotted, his cock pushed at the confines of his jeans. He was a rock, but she was the stream, running gently, soothingly over him. So much, he wanted to dive right in.

Deep in, the coyote in him growled.

While his body raced away on wild fantasies, screaming for the woman at his side, his brain muddled along in a fog. He was stuck, immobile, unable to react.

Off-limits, his mind said. *She's way, way off-limits.*

That didn't stop his heartbeat from spiking as she inched closer, though.

Thunder rattled the windowpanes, yet the tickle of her breath on his ear had a greater impact on him. He struggled to keep his breathing steady, not to give anything away. Why did he feel so out of control?

Because she's so close. The coyote grinned inside.

So close that every rivet in his mental armor was creaking under the pressure to break free.

Take her! Take her now! his wolf howled.

In that moment, it was easy to believe the old stories. That there really was such a thing as a destined mate. Not that destiny had spent a lot of time visiting Twin Moon Ranch in the past century, or so much as spat in his direction. But maybe the drought was over. Maybe even a guy like him—a mutt, the product of an empty union—could get that lucky.

Lightning flashed, illuminating the harsh truths concealed amidst the desert landscape. He could see them cowering out there. Truth, like the fact that a life lived alone was empty. Truth, that good enough was not enough, not for his restless soul.

Truth, that the path to his future lay not in the barrens but at his side. His future was her.

For all that lightning tried to tell one tale, though, thunder told a different story. Each roar was like the stomp of an insistent foot.

Duty! Duty!

Every member of the pack had a duty and Zack knew his. He was supposed to bring Rae back to the ranch. To protect her, not get carried away with crazy ideas.

"Zack," she whispered, running a hand over his shoulder.

She seemed hell-bent on encouraging those crazy ideas, though. It was in her whisper and the warm slide of her hand along his chest. He'd sensed her wrestling with indecision earlier, but now she seemed to have made up her mind. Didn't she get the memo about the kid from the wrong side of the ranch?

Apparently not, his coyote chuckled as she wiggled closer, making him feel impossibly good. As good as she'd made him feel on that glorious bike ride. He'd tasted freedom, purpose, and companionship, all on two wheels. Those forty-five minutes might have been the high of his life, what with her wrapped around him like a lining to his jacket.

You think that was a high? his coyote sneered. *Try this.*

Before he realized it, his hand slid around her waist, and sure enough, her body shuddered with delight that echoed through him.

This is the way to get high, his wolf agreed as he tugged her closer.

Her hand settled over his heart while her lips played along his jaw, licking him up. She'd fought her inner battle and won; why couldn't he do the same?

The harder his cock grew, the more his wolf came up with lame excuses why this would be all right.

Ty only said something about keeping other guys from messing around with her, right?

Logic had never been the beast's strong point. Had it forgotten that Ty's father, the pack alpha, had also warned Zack to stay away from Rae?

Still, the coyote was mesmerizingly persuasive.

This isn't messing around, the beast promised in a silky, sure tone. *This is destiny. Not even the old man can fight that.*

And hell, it certainly felt that way. Every cell in his body seemed to lean toward Rae, and the urge he felt was as much a directive to hold her forever as to bury himself in her body.

She wants us, too!

That, Zack had to give the wolf. The woman who refused to flutter her feathers for any man was melting fast — for him! Her gray eyes were glassy with desire. For all that she'd been on guard with him, she'd reached the conclusion that this was worth it. He was worth it.

His heart gave a little sputter, then hammered on.

She tugged on his chin, turning his face to hers. "I'm declaring it open season on trackers. Fair warning."

He wanted to smile at that, and a lot of other sweet things about her, but his facial muscles were too stiff.

"I can't kiss you," he heard himself say, even though he leaned forward. He might as well put the rule he was about to break out there for the record, right? Maybe that would lessen the guilt, if the guilt ever came.

"I can't *not* kiss you," she insisted.

A flash of lightning revealed the landscape, and it was different than the familiar view of home. A reminder of just how far away the ranch and its rules were.

Zack hauled in a deep breath. How long had it been since he'd taken a risk? How long had since he'd cared enough to dare?

Too long, his coyote howled.

So, dare. Risk. Kiss, his wolf urged.

Rae closed the distance, letting her lips cover his. Slowly, he locked his arms around her and pushed everything else away.

He'd been fighting the attraction with everything he had because this woman was to arrive back on Twin Moon Ranch untouched. She was forbidden. That was as clear as the ivory fangs the old alpha had flashed when he'd interrupted their first kiss. Zack was entrusted with her well-being. He couldn't fail in the one sliver of trust afforded him by the old alpha. For her sake, and his own.

But for once, he didn't want to settle for playing the good beta. He wanted to jump right to the top, where he belonged. To take destiny in his hands, not wait for it to come to him.

A man could spend a lifetime waiting, and he had had enough.

Finally, he closed his eyes on duty and opened his lips to hers.

That kiss should have been an explosion of sound and color and lust, for all that his wolf had been straining to have Rae. But it was soft, cushiony, and restrained. Lingering, as if every second represented a lifetime. Trusting, with more than just the physical. The kind of kiss he'd had only once before—the one with her, back on the ranch.

Lightning and thunder receded until all he heard was the tame crackle of a fireplace sparkling a cozy vision to life: a bowl of popcorn, two pairs of intertwined feet, and a couple of carefree lovers wrapped around each other atop a thick rug.

All that in one kiss. Either this was destiny or he was losing his mind.

Whatever it was, he had no choice but to go along for the ride. No seat belt, no helmet, no rules.

No limits, something in him agreed. *Not tonight.*

Rae's soft touch took him from the fireplace to a sunny mountaintop with a miles-wide view over a landscape carpeted in the colors of spring. Hope bloomed all around. In his imagination, the two of them lingered there a little while. Then they ambled to a hollow filled with the white fleecy fluff of cottonwood trees, so thick it came right up to his ankles. Rae pulled him onward, toward his little shack out by the mesa on the ranch and the bed inside.

Then his hands were hitting a mattress on either side of her body, and he was transported back to this remote cabin in the hills, far, far from watchful eyes on the ranch. It was real. She was real. And her need was as great as his.

"Zack," she whispered, pulling him closer.

He lowered himself, keeping his weight half an inch above her body, as if he might squeeze the goodness out of this if he went too fast. For once, he didn't want to lose himself in a woman. He wanted to find himself there.

Her hands traveled up his shirt and her fingers played along his spine just the way he'd imagined: the index finger first, callused and stimulating, then the middle finger, smooth and long. After that came the softer ring finger, and finally the pinkie, barely a brush.

He wanted to hum and tell her to do it again, but all that came out was a grumble.

His coyote sighed in exasperation. *Can't you get anything right?*

I'm trying!

Try harder, his wolf muttered.

"No good?" Her eyebrows shot up.

"Very good," he assured her, pulling her hand back into place. He said it again, ironing out the kinks in his voice, just for her. "Very good."

Rae turned on a smile that was all cheek and only a little lip, like she was trying to hold it back. Then her clever fingers found the hem of his shirt and pulled it over his head. A breath later, she was wiggling under him, pulling her own top and bra off, and then settling back.

He held his breath, and his coyote sighed inside. *Very good.*

His eyes raked her torso, a masterpiece of mixed art forms. The cubist planes of her abdomen melted into the soft, impressionist curves of her breasts, then swept up the length of her neck to the chiseled planes of her face.

Your turn, her eyes grinned.

Zack felt the wolf rear up inside, body-checking the man and coyote aside. The beast's hungry eyes locked on the prize, declaring all bets off. It was definitely his turn. And if there were any rules to this game, he was about to blow them to tiny bits.

Chapter Twelve

With all the electricity in the air, Rae expected a breathless tussle, a rush to fulfillment, the burst of a dam. But even after their lips met, Zack devoted a long time to nuzzling, staking his claim. The way he touched her suggested that sex came way down on a very long list that put worshiping and discovery above everything else.

She was the one turning up the heat. It was her, pressing her hips to his. It was her, guiding him back to the bed until he had no choice but to ease her into position beneath him. Even then, his kisses were slow and sultry, like a dance on a long winter's night. He seemed in no rush to peel off her layers, to get underneath.

Very un-wolf-like, she decided. And very, very good.

Nuh-uh, her wolf countered. *This man is all wolf. Wait and see.*

She pulled off his shirt, then her own, eager for flesh to meet flesh. That's when the beast flashed in his eyes, making her breath hitch. She saw impatient wolf paired with cunning coyote who was calculating how long he might stretch this night. Animal eyes that promised hot, pulsing passion and steel-hard muscle primed to take.

He dipped his head, found her left nipple, and sucked it into his mouth, gentle despite the raw need pulsing off him. Her nipple peaked, and she could already sense what a satisfied mess she would be before the night was through. She was whimpering already, crying under the stimulation of his tongue and fingers.

She arched back, completely at his mercy, and her wolf howled in glee. The irony wasn't lost on her: the girl who refused to give any man an inch was suddenly handing herself over in yards. But hey, if she was going to dive off the high board, she'd do it with style. Zack was like no man she'd ever met. Alpha, but all heart. Wounded, yet giving. Passionate, but controlled.

Mine, her wolf growled. *All mine.*

The muscles of his shoulders and arms were edgy, like a sculptor had been in a hurry to finish his statue or just given up on hacking at stone that hard. She ran a hand down the landscape of his stomach, diving under his unbuttoned jeans and toward his groin. When her fingers found his shaft and closed slowly over it, she couldn't help a little chuckle.

"Gotcha."

"That was my line," he mumbled.

"Mine now."

All mine, her wolf purred as she worked him slowly up and down.

He groaned into her chest and lay panting, motionless.

Relish, she told herself. *Do not devour.* If any man deserved it, it was him.

He tilted his head up, eyes seeking out hers, and there it was again, that secret, boyish smile. When she raised her free hand to cup his cheek, he leaned into her touch, humming as she explored him from base to tip.

"Promise me you don't bring all the ranch girls here on the back of your bike."

His eyes popped open. "I don't. Never." His voice was raspy, and she believed him. He shook his head and kissed her. "Never."

A clap of thunder brought on a flurry of hasty activity, the two of them rushing to tug off the last layers separating them. But even when her clothes lay flat on the floor and her hands gripped the headboard while her knees spread wide, Zack was tender and slow. A man in a museum, getting it exactly right.

Using his fingers, he explored her folds and tunneled slowly inside, working her in languid circles until she was wide, wet, and crying for more. He shifted his weight, and she was sure she knew what was coming next. He'd line his body up with hers, lock his hips over hers, and slide home at last. Then they would rock, roll, and howl their pleasure into the night.

But what Zack did next, no man had ever done to her before. He sat back, lifted her hips, and pulled her knees to his shoulders in one swift move. She couldn't understand why it felt so right to lie back and let him, but something in her demanded this feeling of being thoroughly and utterly taken.

Claimed? the voice of warning sounded, muffled deep inside.

The raging heat in her smothered the worry right away. Tonight, she would not be denied—especially by herself. It was all about trust. His hung before her like a fragile thread, begging for reinforcement. What choice did she have but to wrap hers around it?

When Zack paused, she could have burst from the pressure building inside. He tipped his head back and breathed deeply, like a weary man on the verge of claiming a hard-fought prize.

Then he swiveled his jaw in a look that said, *Make ready for me, my mate.* Finally, he lifted her to his mouth like a meal too good to leave on the plate.

Her eyes rolled back in their sockets as he feasted on her, his tongue ravishing every fold, every hidden corner of her sex. The action drove her deeper and deeper into a fog bank of bliss. The man consumed her so thoroughly, so eagerly, that all she could do was ride the exquisite movement of his tongue. Her head fell limp against the mattress—the pillow was long gone, a casualty of their movements—and listened to her own moans fill the cabin as she came undone. Higher and higher, tighter and tighter, until every muscle clenched and shuddered.

Zack held her as she came, shaking and howling inside, then fluttered slowly back to earth.

Heaven, her wolf sighed.

She wanted to say something, but her legs were already wrapping around his waist, guiding him home. Hitting the orgasm of her life suddenly wasn't enough; she wanted all of him.

His green eyes studied her, glittering with need.

Need. Not greed. The man was a prince.

"Zack, please." She was begging, but it was better than what her wolf was yowling inside.

Fuck me. Fill me. Now.

Another man might have reveled in the power he held over her, but Zack simply nodded, like her wish was his command.

His green eyes narrowed as he pushed in, one delicious inch at a time. She was consumed by the slick, white heat of him, stretching her, tapping something deep in her soul. This was as emotional as it was physical, and she feared what it might make her say, vow, or promise. Her wolf was trying to bare her fangs and lick his neck in preparation for a mating bite, desperately thirsty for more.

Mate! Mine! her wolf cried, and she swore she could hear his reply.

Mate! Mine!

With a mighty crack, lightning split a tree outside, and the sound boomed over the hills. Zack hammered home then started pumping to a steady beat. Out, and slowly back in. Out, back in. Rae succumbed to the climax coiling inside like a spring, feeling it slip out of her grasp even as she tried to grab on and yoke it back. Zack's pace went from strong and steady to deep and desperate as he, too, gave in to instinct. When he came with a low grunt, she found herself flying, then floating through space, her brain on standby as her body hung on through wave after wave of pleasure.

Then she was nestled beside him, listening to his heart race. Two thick arms wrapped around her: protecting, not possessing. Promising.

Even his sweat smelled clean. Honest. She burrowed against his skin, wondering if she could ever get enough of him.

She hung there, suspended between dreams and conscious thought, marveling at this sense of peace filling the cabin. She could lose herself in dreams. Lose herself in plans, in hopes. But lose herself in a man? It seemed foolish and foolhardy.

Yet it seemed so right.

Chapter Thirteen

Deep in the night, Rae's eyes popped open. She lay still, struggling to comprehend what was tugging at her.

It wasn't Zack, not this time. They'd been up twice already, each time finding another way to dance into each other's arms and bodies, and each time as good as the first. She wouldn't be surprised if her skin was glowing like a beacon in the night. A beacon for him to find his way home to.

Right now, though, Zack's steady breath and relaxed limbs signaled sleep. She watched his chest rise and fall with every breath. Was there anything more appealing than a rock of a man babied by sleep? Especially a man whose moments of peace were as fleeting as his.

She was tempted to brush the hair back from his forehead, to smooth a hand over his skin. But the force urging her awake was a different one. It came from beyond their intertwined limbs, beyond the cabin. From out in the night.

Time to hunt, came the whisper, the call.

Part of her wanted to jump up and obey, while the other part didn't want to budge. She glanced down at her naked body, locked under the weight of Zack's arm. Feeling possessed wasn't supposed to feel so good.

That was the frightening part: she wanted it. She wanted to be possessed.

She told herself she couldn't give in, not even to Zack's wounded warrior appeal. A man like him could take away her freedom and smother her soul. She'd seen it happen again and again. Greer, the brutal alpha in Colorado had been like that. Roric in Nevada had the same heavy-handed style, as did Tyrone of Twin Moon Ranch. His son, Ty, seemed decent enough, but he had that same inner power — so much that it created a black hole all around him.

Alphas were like that. They were all the same.

Even Zack. He kept his power under wraps, but it would snuff her out if she stayed too close for too long. He'd erase the special part that was Rae and shape her into just another mistress. Whether that happened through brute force or her own dumb cooperation, the end result would be the same. She'd lose who she was. Lose everything.

No, her wolf insisted. *Our mate gives without taking away.*

He's not our ma— Rae wanted to insist, but somehow, she couldn't form the words, not even in her mind.

She gave herself an inner shake. *New moon. Time to go.*

Her wolf nodded in agreement. *New moon. Time to hunt.*

The storm was clearing, and Zack had chased Jed away. No reason to wait.

She slid slowly out from under Zack's arm and padded silently to the door, where she hesitated, looking at her bow. Would it be that kind of hunt?

She considered, testing the air. No. Not tonight. Tonight was a wolf hunt. The best kind.

Still, gravity seemed to double its pull on her feet, trying to coax her back to bed. Just further proof, she knew, of what she had to beware of.

Outside, she studied the sky. The storm was clearing quickly, heading south in search of a new stage for its mighty show. The first gaps were appearing between clouds, each twinkling with a pale star. Bit by bit, Rae cleared the clutter from her mind and focused on the task ahead of her. The hunt. It was her duty. Her passion. Her calling.

She closed her eyes and let the moon pull the wolf out of her. Her shift started with a yawn that gave way to a stretch as another body emerged from inside. It came willingly, her body folding into its familiar second shape smoothly. She dropped to all fours and curved her back as golden brown fur broke out over her skin. Her nose stretched long, filling with desert scents while her eyesight faded to grayscale. Her wolf sniffed and whisked its tail, left, then right.

Free at last.

The first scent to stand out—jump out, was more like it—was Zack's, and she fought the urge to hurry back inside. She tilted her nose higher to catch more distant scents, slowly honing in on her prey. There—there it was. Warm-blooded. Musky. Meaty. Something young and healthy. Something strong.

She drew the scent deep into her lungs until it practically circulated in her bloodstream and she could imagine a dotted line snaking over the lumpy landscape to her quarry. Then she shook her furry body and set off on her hunt.

Hunt. A term that was frequently misunderstood—especially her kind of hunt.

Only certain hunts involved killing, and sometimes that task fell to her—to cull the weak and send their bodies back to the earth, their spirits back to the sky. That kind of prey often succumbed quickly, even gratefully. That's what her bow was for—to deliver a quick and merciful end.

Tonight, though, would be a different type of hunt, and it wasn't about killing. It was the trickiest kind of hunt because catching prey alive and uninjured was a far greater challenge.

Rae set off at a trot, ears perked, eyes wary. She would have one chance to get this right.

She settled into a long lope, trying to foresee how tonight's hunt would unfold. Her prey might flee, or it might fight—anything to stay safe. If only her prey knew what was best for it, her life would be a lot easier.

Her wolf pulled its lips back in a grin. *Now, what fun would that be?*

One mile stretched into two, then three, as she wound through the scrubby terrain, closing in on her prey. Her paws pounded over dirt and rock, nose high in the air. Zack's style of tracking would be different: nose to the ground as he traced his quarry by following their trail. Hers involved teasing her prey's location out of the myriad scents in the air and closing in on them. That meant she could take shortcuts without fear of losing the trail. But it had to be a fresh and active scent for that to work. A tracker like Zack, on the other hand, could follow older trails, and over longer distances.

We'd be a good team, her wolf decided.

She pushed the thought away. Hunting was a solitary occupation, right?

Wasn't always that way, her wolf grumbled. *In the old days—*

Rae cut it off there. Yes, she'd heard the stories of the glory days, when entire packs would join the hunt and run as one in the night. But those days were gone. Her kind had become as rare as the species it was her job to protect, and group hunts even more rare.

Still, it felt good to be out running in the night, even alone. Her heart pounded and her claws skittered over ground. She raced up a rocky mesa then padded to a stop and crept over a ridge. Below her, a tight little valley with a tall line of trees followed the meandering path of a stream. She could smell fresh water and the lush scent of the plants sucking it all in.

There. Her quarry was there, in the shadows below.

It was drinking from the stream in short sips, popping its head up regularly to scan the area before ducking down to drink again. Its movements were barely perceptible in the gray-on-black shadows, but once Rae had honed in on it, the shape grew clear.

A pronghorn. A magnificent desert pronghorn, one of the rarest of the rare. The pure white of its rump flashed against the landscape, while the darker lines accenting its curves blurred its edges, making it a mere ghost in the night. A female. Young, sturdy, and very much on edge.

As the doe should be. The few pronghorns left in the wild were valued by trophy hunters for their beautiful pelts and one-of-a-kind horns. They'd been hunted to near-extinction before making a tenuous recovery—but who knew? Every individual was critical to the species' survival—especially a young female like this.

Except it was too early in the season for the gazelle-like creature to be in this neck of the desert. What was the silly doe thinking?

Sadly, pronghorns weren't known for their brains.

She'll be fast, though. Her wolf licked its lips. *Fast enough to give a good chase.*

Therein lay the challenge. A wolf would have to be clever *and* fit to catch a pronghorn like this.

Watch me, her wolf grinned.

She pressed her belly to the ground and let the earth's heat seep into her body as she formulated a plan. She'd circle and approach from the west, sticking to the thick line of scrub flanking the trees. Then she'd—

A twig snapped on her right and the desert went deathly still. The pronghorn flicked its ears—once, twice—then fled.

Rae cursed and whipped her head toward the intruder: a coyote, just coming over the rise. He'd been quiet, but not quiet enough.

No, not a coyote. A wolf. Or was it a coyote?

Something in between, she decided. A very sexy something with the imposing size of a wolf and the coloring of a coyote.

Zack?

She hated that part of her gave a happy zing to see him. The other part, however, couldn't help a yelp of protest. He was ruining her hunt!

She took off after her quarry, claws scuttling over the earth while her wolf lodged an entire catalog of complaints.

Stupid man! Stupid tracker! Stupid... Then the memories kicked in. *Sexy man. Sexy tracker. Sensitive lover...*

Enough! The hunter in her roared and concentrated on the chase. She could hear Zack tearing through the brush behind her; no reason for stealth now. Her ears flicked forward, concentrating on the pronghorn. She had to get it!

The pronghorn was fast but foolish in its panic. It crashed through the thicker scrub along the creek bank while Rae pounded a parallel path in the clearer ground above. She stretched her muzzle forward, lengthening her stride to keep pace with this fleet-footed doe.

The chase stretched on, over rocks, gullies, and hills. Rae lost herself in the sensations: the desperate hoofbeats over dry earth, the rhythm of her pounding heart, the sound of her fellow wolf close behind.

At first she'd been annoyed. What was Zack thinking, coming after her like this? But having him involved in the hunt added to the thrill. She'd done all her hunting alone, and while she'd never felt lonely, she'd also never felt so connected to her own kind.

In the old days... her wolf started.

Yes, she'd heard about the old days, when wolves hunted in packs and tended their territories as one. They kept the herds strong by culling the weak, the old, and the sick. In return, the herds kept the wolves fed. It was an ageless, symbiotic relationship that ensured balance and survival of both species—and a responsibility still honored by hunters like her.

Rae ran as she'd never run before, tuned in to both her quarry and to Zack. To share the thrill of the hunt... There was a certain rightness to it.

Her mind spun as her limbs continued the chase. If the hunt was once a pack affair, then...

Her ears flicked back to Zack. Did he know anything about her kind of hunting? Would he know how to work in tandem to bring down their prey—not to kill it, but to send it on a better path?

She flipped through a hundred possible scenarios. Could she trust him?

In an instant, her decision was made. All or nothing. She cut sharply to the right, up the hillside. Could she trust Zack?

There was only one way to find out.

Chapter Fourteen

Jesus, but the she-wolf could run. That pronghorn, too.

Zack panted and searched for another gear to throw his four feet into, but he was already going flat out. He ought to feel guilty for scaring off her prey, but hell, he'd still been half asleep when he came across them. And anyway, Rae was the one who'd walked out on him in the middle of the night.

A night he'd thought was perfect, until he woke up alone.

He couldn't believe it at first. A couple of rounds of intense sex, a quick cuddle, and Rae had made tracks.

Well, maybe she was smart to do so. After all, a man like him couldn't offer much: just a shack on the edge of the ranch, a crazy job, and an uncertain pedigree. The only thing he could really offer was his heart, and that was worn as thin as an overused couch.

Still, it hurt. Bad. That feeling of being left behind was an old one, and the pain went further back than a couple of hours. It went back years. Lots of them.

One night, his father would be home, the warm bass of his voice filling the house. The next, a motorcycle engine would roar to life, carrying an impatient man out of a young boy's life. Every couple of months, his dad would drop in, looking clean, repentant, and deceptively sincere—a state that would last just long enough for Zack to save up a little hope. Long enough for it to sting when the man disappeared again. In and out, in and out, with little Zack hiding beneath his patchwork quilt, afraid to fall asleep for fear of who might come—or worse, who might go. Wondering what it might be like to hear an engine coming instead of going.

He'd pushed the memories away for so long that when they came back, they came back with a bang.

At first, he'd sat slumped on the bed, kneading his brow and wondering at when his subconscious had decided that things could be different. Where had the wild ideas come from? Ideas like sleeping long, solid, and off guard, knowing that he'd have a person he loved for more than one night.

He caught himself there. He wasn't a kid any more, and as for love—no, he didn't love Rae. More like...liked her. And he'd had his fun, so what more did he want?

More, his wolf whimpered, morose. *Mate. Keep.*

Forever, the coyote added.

He shook his head. He couldn't love Rae. It was forbidden. This whole night had been a mistake.

Coyote and wolf voices roared in his head. *No mistake!*

He'd been planning to feel sorry for himself a while longer, but his nose had started twitching. There was something was in the air, and not just the scent of regret. Some nocturnal event; something exciting. His hands fisted in the sheets. Was Rae in danger? Was Jed back?

He leaped to his feet, flung the door open, and shifted to canine form, senses on full alert while scents and sounds assaulted him.

The new moon. The desert, caught between two breaths. Something was happening out there.

He paced on the porch, sniffing. Where was Rae?

Like needles on a thousand tiny compasses, every sensor in him swung north. There. She was there. Somehow, he just knew. He took off at a punishing pace, tracking her fresh scent through the night. It wasn't long before anger and pain gave way to the thrill of the chase. There was a high in it, running through the cool night air. His legs were strong and sure as they carried him over the hill, around a mesa, up over a rise—

Where two heads had popped up in surprise. He let out an inner curse. *Shit.*

One was the slender face of a pronghorn—a doe with wide eyes, erect ears, and inward curving horns. The other was a she-wolf with a silky brownish-gold coat, long legs, and an aristocratic tilt to her chin.

Rae yipped her displeasure at the noise he made then shot off after the pronghorn.

The promise of a double chase pushed away any instinct Zack had to hang his head in shame. The pronghorn was taking off, Rae was taking off, and dammit—he was off, too. He would not be left behind!

So there he was, running with his paws on fire, his teeth clenched in resolve. But damn if the two females weren't giving him a run for his money. He caught glances of the pronghorn's thin legs pistoning up and down, its flag of a tail flicking as it ran in great leaps and bounds. The doe was running on high-octane fuel: fear for her life.

Rae, on the other hand, ran on the wings of some desert spirit. There was an aura about her, a glow. Her coat shouldn't shimmer quite so much on a moonless night, but there it was, flashing over the landscape like a golden fish in murky water. He'd never seen a wolf move like that: a tight package of grace, determination, passion, and pure feminine power.

Oh, but you have seen that, his coyote hummed. *And not too long ago.*

He nearly stumbled when the image jumped into his mind: Rae, tugging him toward the bed between flashes of lightning. Rae, lying back and inviting him to explore. Rae, writhing in pleasure as he thrust into her, again and again.

His inner thermometer jumped by twenty degrees. OK, so the two of them had been on fire. But that was only sex, right?

His coyote snorted. *Who else ever lit you on fire? Who else ever made you feel so alive?*

He thought long and hard but came up empty. Worse, he was lagging behind. He pushed the thoughts out of his mind, determined not to lose contact with the chase.

But there was determination, and there was sheer inborn speed. His tongue lolled sideways out of his mouth while the females showed no signs of tiring. If anything, they were inching away. The pronghorn had two hundred yards on Rae, who had half that distance on him. And Christ, he wasn't sure he could catch them, not even at a full-out sprint.

Then his she-wolf suddenly cut off at an angle and hammered upslope, away from the pronghorn. He slowed, torn in two different directions. What was Rae doing?

His ears flicked, picking up a whisper in the night. By the time it wound its way into his mind, though, it was more image than sound. If he stayed behind the pronghorn, then drove it right...

An entire scene played out in his mind. If he edged left, the doe would veer right. And if Rae was fast enough, she could cut over the hilltop and cut the pronghorn off on the other side.

We hunt as a pack, the whisper told him. *Like the old days.*

Zack wasn't sure what those old days were, but he grinned and shot off after the pronghorn.

Clever, his human side decided.

Insulting, his wolf huffed. *She wants us to play sheepdog?*

Cunning, the coyote smiled. *She does her part, we do ours.*

It was two against one, because the man in him was with the coyote: smitten with the challenge. And hell, he'd never been on a hunt like this before. Tracking was in his blood, but that was slow and steady, his nose testing every inch of earth before moving on. This was a high-speed chase with whipping branches, crashing hoofbeats, and pounding hearts. This was thrilling, instinctual. The only times he'd been out on this kind of hunt had been frivolous, opportunistic chases of a wayward deer or boar. A pronghorn was in a totally different class, especially one as fleet as this.

Rae was in a totally different class, too. She carried her nose straight as an arrow, her tail proud as a banner.

His wolf wasn't sure he liked the arrangement, though.

Aren't men supposed to lead and women to follow? Shouldn't an alpha fight from the front and force victory with raw power?

The coyote laughed the notion aside. *Hate to point it out to you, but we're bringing up the rear. And the view ain't half bad.*

He watched Rae disappear into the scrub from the corner of his eye as he followed the pronghorn. Maybe there were other ways to achieve a goal. Maybe a smart alpha knew when to lead and when to follow.

His eyelid twitched, the wolf in him uneasy. *Me, a sheepdog?*

His coyote snorted. *Pompous fucking wolf.*

He swung left, decision made. If Rae wanted a sheepdog, he'd give her one. He took a deep breath, lifted his muzzle, and let out a howl as he raced along. A good howl that rumbled and threatened a thousand bloody deaths. Of course, running at full tilt like that, it was more hot air than anything else. A wolf would never fall for that bullshit, but a pronghorn...

Sure enough, the doe skittered right, just where he wanted her to go.

Zack bayed and yipped, putting on a show that filled him with childish pleasure, just like the kind he got from revving his Harley at a red light.

And it worked. The doe went wide-eyed in panic and drifted right, still a good hundred yards ahead. It was a gap his burning lungs would never close. But it didn't matter, because there was a flash of gold and a grunt on his right. Rae came flying through the air like a Valkyrie straight out of hell. She pounced, and wolf and antelope went rolling in a flurry of flailing hooves, wild grunts, and gleaming teeth.

Zack's heart seized. One lucky kick and the pronghorn could crush Rae's ribs, smash her head, or put out an eye. There was nothing certain about a hunt. Shifters healed quickly, but they weren't immune to pain. Besides, a lucky kick would let the pronghorn escape, and something about Rae's urgency told him that couldn't happen tonight.

When he was two steps away, the tussle came to an abrupt stop, and he skidded to a halt. What the hell was going on?

Rae had the pronghorn pinned as sure as any cowboy threw a steer. Her jaws were clamped around its neck, her body forcing the doe down. She huffed through her teeth, ordering her quarry to submit. He could see the panicked whites of the pronghorn's eyes roll, its striped flanks heave in terror.

But there was no death bite, no gush of blood. Rae wasn't killing the doe; she was holding it. There was a grunt and a wiggle and then silence as the pronghorn's eyes registered something else. It ceased the struggle and just... listened.

Zack listened, too, tilting his head. There was a whisper in the air, faint as filtered starlight from a thousand light-years away. A whisper that carried images, not words, and a scene formed in his mind.

There was a brokeback mountain, a crooked stream, and a wide, green valley swimming in grass. Somewhere up north. Not that he'd ever been there; he just knew. Next, he saw a rocky outcrop, an irregular hillside, and a flash of white: the tail of another pronghorn. A big male, by the look of it.

There, the image seemed to be telling the doe. *That is where you must go.*

Rae loomed over her prey, forcing it to listen to that whisper that rose out of the ground. Then the images rushed into a blur in a bird's-eye flyover of the route to that special place.

Zack sat down abruptly, hitting rocky ground with a jolt of realization.

Holy shit.

He'd heard the legends, of course, but never imagined they were true. Legends of a great huntress with speed and stamina to match any prey. A huntress who guarded the creatures roaming her territory, keeping the herds—and by extension, her pack—healthy. The kind of hunter who tended the earth and maintained a natural balance thrown badly off-kilter in modern times.

The pronghorn struggled to its feet, wobbled a few steps, and dropped its head in exhaustion. There wasn't a drop of blood on its pelt; Rae had been careful. Then the doe gave a clicking kind of grunt and trotted off into the night, heading for the green valley in the north where she would find her mate.

Mate, came a faint echo from his wolf.

His eyes settled on Rae, who had eased into a sitting position and was studiously licking her paw. Most shifter packs—wolf and coyote—had master hunters. But a master huntress... His mind fumbled for the term he'd heard whispered, long ago.

Mistress... Mistress of the Hunt. She who tended the herds as a servant of Mother Earth.

It had been generations since a true huntress had walked the earth. So long that the Mistress of the Hunt had fallen into the realm of legend.

But it wasn't a legend. It was true.

It was Rae.

He lowered his head slowly with a reverent huff.

Rae. His Rae. Mistress of the Hunt.

Chapter Fifteen

Rae watched the pronghorn disappear into the night.

Godspeed, my friend. Good luck. She pushed the thought, loud and clear, from her mind to the doe's, then dropped her chin. The usual post-hunt high washed over her like a drug: she felt weary, yet triumphant. Humble, yet all-powerful. So much of her life was lived at the whim of an alpha's command; this was her chance to run free, to sing her song.

A rare chance, too. Soon, this magical night would be over, and she'd be back to just plain Rae, hiding her secret, fretting about her future.

At least it had been a successful hunt. Rewarding, too: that pronghorn was on its way to a safer place and one of her own kind. If Fate smiled on the doe, she would find her mate, breed, and add another generation to a long, beautiful line.

Rae was one in a long and even rarer line. She sensed the connection during every hunt: a link to her grandmother, great-grandmother, and so many others, so long ago. They'd come to the New World in centuries past to tend once-plentiful herds: bison, antelope, elk. But even the great huntresses couldn't hold back the relentless onslaught of pioneers and trophy hunters. All they could do was guide the last survivors to safe havens where they might hide and persevere.

Part of her itched to give chase to the pronghorn once more, while another part was glad to see it run free. Hope rang in its footsteps, and who knew? Maybe there was hope for Rae, too.

She sighed and bent her head to lick a paw trampled in the fight. Zack was watching, but she wasn't quite ready to face him. Having him join the hunt had given her a thrill that a hundred brass horns couldn't provide. The thrill of leading others on a hunt, just like her grandmother had said.

A little like the old days. Her wolf smiled.

Well, it was a long way from the old days, but she'd take what she could get. If only she could hunt openly with a pack that appreciated her gift. Unfortunately, such packs were few and far between. Roric's Westend pack couldn't give a damn about balance; their souls were sold to the casinos. Other packs might value a huntress like her, but there was a danger in that, too. The wrong kind of pack would rein her in, tie her down. She needed to range wide and far in search of worthy prey, something packs today with their splintered territories would hardly support. If the wrong pack claimed her, she would be reduced to hunting sheep or javelina when her blood called for the rarest of the rare—bighorn, pronghorn, and other species toeing the thin line between survival and extinction.

And now, Zack knew her secret. What if he gave her away?

Rae growled, pushing her human anxieties away. Tonight—what there was left of it—was for celebrating small triumphs: a successful hunt, and a single doe on her way to safe territory and a mate.

Mate.

On cue, her wolf turned to Zack. His green eyes were deep and honest. Wolf, coyote, or human: a trio in one, who looked at her in wonder and surprise, then dipped his head in respect.

Something primal in Rae stirred, and she wanted it again: that feeling of being worshiped—not as a Mistress of the Hunt, but as an ordinary woman who couldn't deny her attraction to this man.

Mine. Mate. Her wolf growled as she stepped toward Zack. He would make a worthy mate. Honest and true. A friend. Who could understand her better than a tracker?

He kept his head low as she circled him.

This hunt is finished, she wanted to say.

But we're not, her wolf grinned, grinding her shoulder against his.

His eyes shone as if he still couldn't believe what he'd seen, so she butted him lightly with her hip. But this time, the contact slowed and stretched until it was a full-body rub along his side. Long, sleek, and close, she slid along the length of his coat. The coyote coloring made him appear smaller from a distance, but he loomed over her now, big as a wolf. Bigger, in fact, than most. She rubbed all the way around him and down the other side, sending up sparks.

When Zack turned his head and his eyes met hers, they said everything. That he was done with the hunt, but only getting started with her.

Heart thumping, she forced herself two steps away and took a measured breath. Hunting brought out her passion, and that passion wasn't easily quenched. In hunts past, she would slip home and find herself a wolf lover to take the edge off. She could do the same now with him. Her wolf wanted it, and his, too.

But tonight... Tonight was different, somehow. She didn't want fast and hard. She wanted slow. Graceful. Satisfying—not just for her body but her soul. And wolves, well, they weren't much good at anything but a hard, fast fuck.

Hey! her wolf huffed.

But her mind was made up. Humans were much pickier about choosing partners. Rae was picky. She wanted Zack—the man.

But would he want her? Would he want slow, graceful, and sweet?

As she looked into the warm peat of his eyes, Zack stood impossibly still. Wishing, wanting, waiting. For her.

And just like that, she slipped from arousal to full heat. She wanted him—all of him, for all of her. She pushed forward, shifting smoothly in midstep to her human form. Her back lifted and straightened, her shoulders stretched, and her jaw clicked. Then she breathed deeply and stood naked on two feet in the desert night. It was cooler like this. Invigorating.

Zack stood still, holding his breath. His wolf stood so tall, she could run a hand along his back without dipping a shoulder. His fur was wiry and thick against her palm, and she couldn't resist working her fingers down to the skin as she circled him once again. She ran the back of her hand along his right side then stepped in front of him, naked and exposed. She shivered, both from the night chill and the primal heat zipping through her body.

Decide, wolf, she strained to tell him as her nipples hardened into tight peaks. *Take me or leave me. Take the risk.*

He blinked, slow and ponderous, and she circled him again. Her hand rose as he shifted and came to two feet, his human side stealing the night back from the beast. Fur gave way to smooth, supple skin as her fingers continued her path, sliding from his hips to a rear so tight and square with muscle that she shivered. She came around his shoulder, a dancer in a slow waltz, and stepped right into an embrace.

Zack—human Zack—pulled her close, nose to her hair, and continued the movement without missing a beat. His arms stroked her the way she had stroked his wolf, making her body throb with building need.

"Rae," he whispered.

He rubbed the pad of his thumb over her lower lip before kissing her exactly as he had the very first time. The scent of wolf hung on him still, and the flavor of coyote was on the tongue that tangled with hers, soft and sweet. Yet he was all human, all man.

She couldn't help glancing down when he reluctantly broke the kiss off. Definitely all man.

He smiled that secret smile, and her knees wobbled just a little bit. She wanted to hand herself over to him, then and there. The hunter in her was gone with her wolf, and now she was all woman. She wanted to surrender, to give herself over to his touch. To trust.

Trust. She turned the word over in her mind. When had she ever really trusted a man?

She closed her eyes and sighed as Zack slid his hands along her ribs, ghosting along the outside curve of her breasts.

Tonight. Tonight she would trust.

His hand cupped her fully, setting her on fire. She pressed into him, trying to squeeze away every last atom between their bodies.

Zack...

It was an inner sigh more than anything else, because speaking now might break the spell of this magical night. Her body cried for more, and he readily gave it, toying with both breasts, pushing his erection into her stomach. Heat pulsed off his chest as his mouth explored hers, swift and sure.

His hands slid down to the small of her back, then climbed up, and finally dove again, scooping her close. So close that her balance was thrown, her body tipping backward.

Trust. The word echoed in her mind as she forced herself to let go. She tipped farther and farther off-balance, so far she was sure she would crash gracelessly to the ground.

"Gotcha," Zack whispered, locking his arms firmly behind her. She felt feather-light as he lowered her to the ground and followed, settling carefully along the length of her body. The rock beneath her was flat and smooth; above, Zack was all heat.

Take me. Love me. Mate me. Her wolf was begging inside, and it was all she could do to lock the words in.

Dipping his head, Zack went to work on her breasts. She arched into his mouth, wanting more of what she'd tasted earlier that night—that screaming, soaring high. The physical high was only one part of it, though. The rest went deeper, sending her soul singing and dancing. Rae wanted to drag this out and make the last hours of the night stretch on forever.

But her body was skipping ahead, making her drop her knees wide and guiding his hand down to stroke her sex. She caught a grin—*Jesus, that smile*—before closing her eyes to the sweet sensation of his fingers tickling her folds. She gasped when his lips grasped her nipple at the same time, bringing her higher and higher. One finger, then two slipped inside her and stirred a moan from her throat.

"Good," she couldn't help whispering. "So good."

Zack's grin stretched, and his green eyes narrowed. Just when Rae was sure he'd nudge her legs wider and push home, Zack took firm hold of her hips and rolled them both around. She reared above him, her knees straddling his hips.

"You want the bottom?" She gaped.

"I want this view."

She sucked in a breath, let it out slowly, then leaned back on her heels to sit tall over his prone body. She tilted her chin up toward the stars. "They are beautiful." The sky was almost free of clouds now, and the stars sparkled in one of those nights of million-mile clarity that only come after a storm. "Like jewels in the sky."

"Not the stars," he murmured. "You. Riding me." He tipped his hips up.

She caught her lower lip in her teeth and formed a triangle over him, one arm on either side of his muscled chest. Then she slid a little higher along his body and lowered herself slowly over his cock.

"Oh!" she cried, taking him deep.

"Oh," he chuckled.

She rocked back, taking him deeper, forcing those perfect lips open in his own silent *Oh*. Gripping her hips tightly, he pushed up, seating himself deep as her inner muscles gripped tightly.

We make a good team, her wolf purred.

That we do, she could have sworn she heard him think, but her mind went blank with his next grinding thrust. She let her muscles ripple over his cock, tightening and loosening in a sensual wave.

His eyes closed while he groaned, long and unsteady, like a rolling log in a swirling river.

"Gotcha." She smiled, liking what she saw.

Zack opened his eyes and found a new grip on her hips, guiding her into another plunge. Down she went, wet, wide, and aching for more. She let her muscles tug on him as she pulled up, hovered over the broad head of him, and pushed down again. She could have played there forever, but a new inspiration seized her. On the next up, she slid her whole body back and away, her breasts bouncing over his thighs as she took his cock with her lips. Not a lazy lick, or a slow glide down. She made a mental oath to deliver that next time. Instead, she rushed to inhale him, extracting another groan from her lover.

Mine. All mine.

She took him again and again until he was slick and swollen, his body motionless but for the fingers twirling madly in her hair and the garbled words pouring from his throat. A rush went through her as the balance of power tipped toward her end of the scale. Of course, power wasn't the point—it was about trust. Zack was trusting her to take him this way—a rare act for a dominant wolf. The question was, how far did her trust go?

Far enough that when he jackknifed up a moment later, rasping her name, she let him take control and roll them until he came out on top, wearing a devilish grin that said, *Watch this.*

Chapter Sixteen

Zack could have thrown his head back and howled when he came out of that roll. Rae was beneath him, wide-eyed and ready for more. She'd given him the ride of his life and now, he would reciprocate, so she'd never want anyone else again. It would be him, only him.

Mine! the wolf inside him roared.

The way her wolf had teased him with those long drags on his fur had nearly been his undoing. But when Rae shifted back to her human form and let her fingers play along his back, his wolf had started humming inside, leaning into the touch. When she circled him the second time, the shift snuck up on him, so smooth and so fast he barely found his balance on two bare feet.

Vague inner warnings like *Forbidden* were forgotten the instant Rae molded herself to his body in a perfect fit. Her trust wasn't given lightly, and that alone was enough to push aside duty and honor and pack. He had to touch her, taste her, fill her.

Her skin was soft and warm, and underneath was a taut layer of muscle: thin as sheet metal in places, corrugated over her abdomen, thicker in the thighs. Thighs that were gripping him now, drawing him in. The thunder and lightning had long since moved on, but he could still feel the electricity in what she did to him. His lips moved over her shoulder, tasting her again and again, and then everything became the squeeze on his cock as he slid home.

He thought he'd climbed as high as a man could climb, but he soared even higher when Rae tipped her chin down to watch his cock disappear inside. Her face glowed as she watched him slide in, one hot, tight inch at a time. Her lips parted, her eyes slid shut, and deep inside, he could feel her tremble.

He wanted to memorize the feel of it all. The sight of her under him. The perfect fit at the juncture of their bodies, the tight tangle of their legs.

He thrust so deep, he nearly lost himself on the first plunge. Rae's eyes were glassy, and he penetrated again, burning with pleasure every inch of the way. A pull back, then another thrust, and another—he let momentum build until the movement was a thing of its own. His breath was ragged, barely in control.

"Zack," she groaned, tightening her legs behind his back.

Mate, his wolf growled inside.

When she clamped down over the length of his cock, all thought fled except the desire to fulfill her.

"Now," she cried.

"Now," he echoed while he still could. Then his hips took over in a crescendo that seemed to rock the stone they lay upon, as hard and fast as an out-of-control wave. It built and crested inside then came in a rush as he emptied into her.

He kept his tight grip on her hips as his body went stiff, feeling Rae clutch him with every muscle and limb. She convulsed with a cry then went limp and breathless against his chest.

Somehow, he found just enough coordination to wrap his arms around her and hold her tight, listening to the wild beating of her heart.

"You're amazing," he murmured at last.

She was so much more than what was visible from the outside. A few minutes ago, she'd been a mighty huntress; now, she was all woman.

All his.

"Not bad yourself," she chuckled back.

Her scent filled his nose, and her heat filled his arms. Their breaths evened out, and time stretched and decelerated, as if Fate were giving him the gift of time.

Mistress of the Hunt. Had he imagined it all? The chase, the pronghorn, the scene that had appeared in his mind? Could a woman like her ever settle for a half-breed like him?

He glanced down, finding stroking him like a harp. She sighed, sinking deeper into him as the stars arched slowly overhead.

"Is this what you came out here for?" He ventured at last. "To hunt?"

She gestured toward the valley, the mesas, the endless miles beyond. "I need space," she said, determination creeping into her voice.

Zack peered into the starry night, wondering how much space she needed. Wondering whether she might be willing to share.

"But you... you held it," he whispered, snuggling her closer in case the words set off her instinct to flee. "The pronghorn, I mean."

Rae shook her head slowly, looking weary, yet satisfied. "Wolves have always been the guardians of the herds. We keep them strong."

He ran a finger over the soft skin of her neck. "Never seen a wolf do that before."

She shrugged and cast her eyes down. "You know that corny line. If you love something, set it free."

But there was more to her hunt than that corny line, and he knew it. "You didn't kill it."

"That pronghorn didn't need killing. She needed..." Rae trailed off, studying him as if to gauge how much to say. "She needed to listen."

"And that's what you do? You tell them where to go?" The image of the green valley had been so clear, he could smell the fresh grass, taste the clean breeze. "Where they'll be safe?"

Rae took a long time measuring her words before speaking. "I don't say anything. The Earth Spirits do. I just make sure she listens."

He nodded. "So she'll know where to go. Where she'll be safe. Where she'll find a mate..." He trailed off, glad Rae's eyes avoided his while he fought down the squeezing sensation in his chest.

The thing was, he didn't need a whisper in the night. He knew where to find his mate.

Right here. His coyote hummed in satisfaction.

Rae cleared her throat and mumbled, "A good hunt."

A very good hunt, his wolf rumbled inside.

"Interesting kind of hunt," he added, trying to keep his voice steady.

Rae pursed her lips. "There's killing, too, when there needs to be. The old, the weak, the sick. Everything has its time. I do it right, though," she continued, sounding fierce. "Quick, and with honor. Not like those damn trappers, the bear-baiters, the humans who get it wrong. They take the strongest bucks, the brightest females."

It all fit perfectly with the stories his grandmother used to tell. But Rae was no coyote. "You're not Diné," he said.

Diné? her eyes asked.

"Navajo."

She shook her head. "My family came from Europe. They couldn't stop humans from decimating the herds there, so they came to the New World. They did their best to keep the herds strong, but others came, too. Too many, too fast."

That story, Zack knew all too well. "Are you the only one?"

Her pulse slowed to a sad thump. "My grandmother was the only huntress in the Four Corners region. The gift skipped a generation with my mom. And me... I'm the only one I know who's... different."

Zack pulled her closer, wishing he could say what he felt: that he knew how it felt to be different, to be alone. But Rae was special, one of a kind. And he was just a mutt.

Try selling that, his coyote cried, suddenly morose.

Chapter Seventeen

To Rae, a night had never felt so good, and dawn had never come so swiftly. She lay snuggled alongside Zack, alternatively snoozing and watching the stars until orange and pink hues invaded the sky.

A new day. What revelations would this one bring?

She rolled to face Zack, matching each part of her body to his, and took his lips in a last kiss. The last, at least, for that night. Then she stood, stretched, and offered him a hand.

He didn't move at first, and she wondered what was going through his mind. He'd gone from passionate and hopeful to downright quiet as the first rays of sunlight tiptoed over the earth.

"Hey." She gave him an encouraging smile. "Time to get up, Sleeping Beauty."

He cracked one eyelid open. "That would be you."

The crazy thing was, he wasn't joking. His fingers closed around hers like he never wanted to let go.

She squeezed and pulled him up. Lying on the ground, they'd come out eye to eye, but standing, he towered over her. There was so much of him, and so much to him. The man was more than a tracker.

This man could be our mate, her wolf said.

She took a deep breath and looked over the hills. It was a long way back to the cabin.

"On foot or...on foot?" she joked.

He flashed the smile she was hoping for, catching her meaning right away. Should they shift into wolf form to cover the miles back or walk on bare human feet?

"Four feet would be quicker." He said it quietly, almost testing her.

"Right, then." She nodded. "Let's go on two feet."

The smile stretched. "Right, then, two feet."

They picked their way through the scrub, cutting over the hill, then winding through the valley where she'd first found her prey. It all seemed so different in daytime and as a human, but one thing was the same: the thrill she got from Zack being there at her side.

Imagine hunting like this all the time. With him.

It was so easy to imagine, and so tempting.

But can we trust him?

Purrr-fectly, her wolf replied, thumping her tail.

Which only brought her to the next question: How much could she trust herself?

The question hung in every prickly pear thorn she tip-toed around and every edgy pebble on the ground. But with Zack's hand tight around hers and his quiet presence at her side, finding a definitive answer didn't feel quite so urgent any more.

They reached the cabin and paused just inside the threshold, gazing at the evidence of their lovemaking. The tangled sheets... The heady musk that still clung to the air. It would be easy, too easy, to slip right back to where they'd left off.

Zack's hand tightened around hers, and he whispered, "We need to get back."

She wanted to stay and pretend that last night could be every night for the rest of her days. But pretending wouldn't get her anywhere, so she scooped up her clothes and dressed. Meanwhile, Zack pulled on his jeans then straightened the bed. She tugged on her shirt then slung her bow and quiver over her shoulders, wishing it wasn't already time to go.

When Zack stepped out the door and pushed the motorcycle off the porch, there was a metallic ting as the keys fell out of his pocket. Rae picked them up as she stepped into the intense morning light, squinting. The night was gone. If she wanted her future, she had to go out and get it.

Zack put out his hand like a catcher's mitt, and she hesitated. Was she ready to put a man in the driver's seat of her life? She jingled the keys, turning the thought over like a tarnished penny.

"You have a motorcycle license, miss?" Zack called.

His tone was joking, but his eyes said, *Give me the keys.* And there it was again—her inner doubt. A bossy alpha was the last thing she needed.

She stiffened slightly. "As a matter of fact, I do."

He studied her then added a lifted eyebrow. *Give me the keys, please.*

She fingered the jagged ridge of the key until her wolf nudged her thoughts. *This man, we can trust.*

She tossed the key chain to him, putting everything into a look that said, *Do not betray my trust.*

Zack tossed her a helmet by way of a promise.

"What about you?" She motioned at the single helmet.

He rapped his fingers on his skull, smiling. "Hard head." Then he started the bike with an easy kick and motioned her onto the back.

With a deep breath, she slid into place. The minute she got in position—chest to his back, legs against his, arms circling his waist—the worries fled. This felt good. Safe. Right.

Home, her wolf murmured.

With a twist of his wrist, Zack revved and took off, and promise shimmered on the horizon. Maybe it wasn't the end of a beautiful night but the start of a beautiful day. Who knew?

Rae leaned into Zack and let herself revel in every turn and every gear he accelerated through. What a car window was to a dog, she decided, a motorcycle must be to a shifter. Her worries blew away with the wind as she gave herself over to the joy of it. Judging by the swell of Zack's lungs under her tight grip, he felt the same. His shoulders went wide and sang of the joy of an open road, of a humming engine, of a woman's arms—his woman's arms—around his waist.

She smiled into his shoulder blades and let her fingers strum the line of his ribs. When he revved past the spot Jed had cornered her in, she turned her head away. She would deal with her broken-down car later. And as for Jed, Zack had scared him off, right?

She wasn't going to let anything ruin this day. And she was damn well going to stretch it out for as long as she possibly could. Why rush back to the ranch?

But the phone vibrated in Zack's pocket when they hit the highway and turned south. Several times, in fact, in what seemed like a series of urgent messages. He pulled over at a roadside diner, took it out, and scowled.

"Shit."

Maybe hiding out at the cabin forever hadn't been such a crazy idea after all.

What? She wanted to yell the question. *What did the message say?*

He glared at the display, glanced at her, then back at the phone. His fingers tightened around it so hard she thought the housing would crack.

"Zack?"

A cloud passed over his face before he punched the phone off for good. *Let them wait,* those green eyes said, screaming defiance.

What was going on?

He stomped into the diner, pulling her with him. "Breakfast."

It wasn't so much an invitation as a declaration, the taking of a stand. Never had she seen the alpha in him come that close to the surface.

But he's holding the power back, her wolf said. *Holding it back, just for us. See what a good mate he would make?*

She squeezed her lips together but didn't protest.

"Coffee?" she asked cheerfully.

"Coffee," he rumbled.

They sat down and lingered over every bite of pancake, every sip of coffee. And if their movements were mechanical at first, the tension gripping Zack's shoulders gradually unwound. Like the storm that had come and gone last night, his mood moved on, and blue skies followed.

Literally. She got back on the bike and tipped her chin to the sky, soaking in the sun. Zack drove under the speed limit, no more eager than she to get back to the ranch. They'd barely gone twenty miles down the road before he pulled over at a scenic overlook where they went straight from taking in the view to taking in each other's lips for another happy minute, or an hour. With him, it was easy to lose track of time.

"This is beautiful," she murmured at last.

"This is nothing," he said, and his secret smile hinted that he knew a better spot.

Sure enough, it wasn't long into the last stretch of road before he swung the bike off the highway at an unmarked juncture. They bumped off-road for half a mile before dismounting and walking to a field of boulders in the shade of a bluff. He pointed to swirls and lines etched into the rock.

"Petroglyphs," she murmured, tracing the air a millimeter above the rock. "Navajo—I mean, Diné?"

He shrugged. "Nobody knows. But there's a feel to this place."

She closed her eyes and tuned in until she felt it—a vibration in the air, like an ancient chant. The whisper of the past. His past?

She opened her eyes on Zack. Coyote, Diné. White man, wolf. Zack had a little of everything in him, and she loved it all.

She stepped closer and hugged him, reaching for his lips to taste what she'd seen. They kissed until their arms started to wander and their tongues reached deeper, when Zack broke off with a start.

"Not here," he whispered, moving away with her hand firmly in his.

Apparently, it was taboo to get heated up in a place as sacred as that. Rae followed her lover silently downslope. A few minutes later, Zack pulled her into a sycamore grove.

"Here," he whispered, picking up where he'd left off.

His hands explored her body, firing every nerve into action, until they'd both stripped and made slow, sweet love as only two destined mates could. By the time the sun was low and they made their way back to the bike, Rae was sure.

Mate. Mine.

She waited a moment for some inner voice of protest, but none came. Those words sounded just right.

Those words are right, her wolf decided.

She could have laughed at herself. There she was, hanging on much tighter than necessary as Zack motored down the highway. The tables had turned, because she wanted to possess him. To keep him, to care for him, to share good and bad and everything in between. And if he wanted to possess her the same way, well, that was a good thing. Especially if he shared the same feeling settling over her now: the one that had her swearing she'd do anything for him.

She closed her eyes and let the wind brush her face. Maybe she didn't have to sell her soul for a man. Maybe she could free it.

"Zack," she called softly, but the wind dragged her voice away.

She wanted to make him pull over so she could tell him what she felt. But they'd already made so many stops and whittled the day away... It really was time to get back to the ranch. The minute they got there, though, she would follow Zack home to his cabin and make sure it was lonely no more.

She smiled into his back, because a day had never been as perfect as this one.

She only snapped out of her thoughts when they rumbled over the cattle grid beneath the ranch gate. Zack's entire body stiffened, and her head popped up to take in the scene. Two words sounded in her mind, and the voice that spoke them was his.

Oh, shit.

Chapter Eighteen

Zack drove straight into a maelstrom more intense than the lightning storm of the previous night. It was in the air, in the guarded faces that greeted them, and in the strange sense of anticipation that cramped his shoulders.

He rolled the motorcycle to a stop. What was going on?

Ty pushed away from where he'd been leaning against the council house, studying the sky for some sign from the gods or some miraculous means of escape. Either would have explained that weary look on his face. When Ty brought his chin down, Zack saw those dark eyes flash between him and Rae.

Whenever Ty was worked up, his eyes packed the power of a punch. And while he was certainly worked up—the set of Ty's jaw was always a dead giveaway, along with his telltale scratching of an ear—tonight seemed different. His eyes mimicked the steady swing of a clock pendulum, solemnly winding up to the hour.

Bong.

The pendulum swung left, and Zack felt that gaze bore into him.

Bong.

It flicked to Rae.

Another silent tick went by, then another heavy bong. Ty's gaze went back to Zack.

Make sure none of the guys dick around with her. The words of the pack's future leader echoed in Zack's mind.

When Ty's gaze swung back to Rae and his nostrils flared, Zack knew he knew. For all that the whipping wind had scoured them on the ride back, the scent of sex remained.

Part of Zack wanted to fold up and slink away, while another part wanted to stand tall and beat his chest. Frozen between the two, he waited for Ty's eyes to ignite, sizzle, and spit. He waited for the pendulum to morph into the sweep of an angry tail on a very ferocious wolf.

But the light in Ty's eyes fizzled away. They only sparked again when old Tyrone stomped over, his eyes overflowing with the rage so strangely absent from his son's face.

When the old alpha's eyes jumped to Zack, he had to fight the instinct to stumble backward. Then those eyes shifted to Rae and went suddenly neutral. Calculating.

Zack looked at the way the old alpha studied Rae, and suddenly, it all clicked.

Rae. A Mistress of the Hunt. A legend reborn.

A legend said to bring prosperity to the lands she tended.

His pulse throbbed through his veins. Somehow, the old man had found out Rae's secret—or he'd known it all along.

Rae hadn't come to the ranch as casual help. She had come to be studied. Verified. A pack that claimed a huntress among its ranks would boom and prosper. She would bring prestige to the pack—and to the family she mated into.

The old alpha's eyes flicked to Ty, and Zack's heart sank to his boots.

Rae had been brought in to be mated to the alpha's son—Ty.

"Where the hell have you been?" Old Tyrone snapped. His head jerked toward the door of the council house. "Inside, now!"

Everything in Zack screamed for him to bundle Rae onto his motorcycle and get the hell away. To rev the engine higher than he'd ever done and race far, far away. But his feet were already shuffling to the council house, pulled by Tyrone's fury and sheer force of habit. His whole life, he'd obeyed the alpha, and habit was a hard thing to break, even with his soul howling inside. It was his duty to serve the pack.

To hell with duty! his coyote cried.

Rae gripped his hand as she moved toward the council house, even though she looked like she wanted to run. Her eyes grabbed his, begging him to keep her secret.

Warn her! Save her! his coyote screamed. *Tell her the secret is already out!*

His wolf, though, had its head down. Duty came above everything else. Everything.

The moment they crossed the threshold, Tyrone slammed the door shut behind them. Then he stalked to the front of the room then spun on his heel. Ty took the spot on his father's right, looking empty and defeated. On the left stood Cody and Tina, the alpha's younger offspring, their lips tightly sealed, clearly wanting no part of what was about to transpire. Beside them stood three of the pack elders, all cronies of the alpha.

Zack knew he had to speak up first, to grab the momentum from the old man. He had never asked the pack for anything, as if he'd been saving up all his wishes for now. For Rae.

He opened his mouth to start, but the old man butted in first.

"You never leave pack territory without permission. You understand me?" he jutted a finger at Rae.

Her lower lip trembled, but she threw her shoulders back and spoke out when any sane person would have withered and crawled away. But that was Rae: brave, ballsy, insistent.

"I didn't leave the territory. I was just exploring."

"You do not go anywhere without my permission. Do you understand, woman?"

Rae held her chin high as the alpha waited for her to submit, her arms crossed in defiance, though trembling.

"Not without my permission—or your mate's," Tyrone continued.

Rae froze. Ty went stiff. Zack's wolf howled inside. A long, mournful howl that echoed through his soul.

"I don't have a mate," Rae half-shouted, beating each syllable for emphasis.

"You will tonight." Tyrone jerked his thumb at Ty.

"No!" Zack growled at the same time that a choked cry popped out of Rae's throat.

"But I don't love him!"

"You'll learn to love him," old Tyrone retorted.

"But I don't want him! I want..." When her eyes shifted to Zack, everyone else's followed.

His lungs pinched as he faced her, straining to catch her next words.

I want you, he thought and waited for her to echo.

But her pupils went wide and she shrank away from him, uttering one word.

"You."

It wasn't the end of a sentence. It was the beginning of an accusation. She trailed off, disgust and betrayal filling her eyes.

"You knew. You told them."

Knew the alpha's plan? Hell no! Told them her secret?

"Never!" His roar went right through the walls of the council house and out over the far corners of the ranch.

"You've done enough!" The old alpha cut him off with a stomp that made the floorboards shake. "And you," he barked at Rae. "You should be grateful!"

But her eyes were still on Zack. Her cheeks were crimson, and her lips tremble with unuttered words. Then she gave a vicious shake of her head and ran out the door.

"Ach," the old alpha grunted. "She thinks she can run."

When Ty moved to follow her, something in Zack snapped. He stepped in front of the alpha's son, blocking his way.

Ty blinked then made to weave around Zack, who sidestepped and put a hand against his friend's chest. He'd had enough. Enough of the old alpha's bullying. Enough of the easy way out. He'd never defied the alpha on anything, never asked for any favor. But it was time to take a stand. Rae was his, and his alone.

Fire began to build in Ty's eyes, and he took hold of Zack's wrist. One flick and Ty would break it.

Then again, one shove and Zack could send Ty stumbling back. They were at an impasse.

"Don't," Zack growled.

Old Tyrone pushed forward. "Get the hell out of the way! My son has a mate to catch!"

Zack couldn't hide the emotion. "She's mine!"

The air in the room trembled the way it would in the split second before the snap of a whip.

"You challenge my son?" The old alpha's face twisted into something between anger and glee.

Challenge Ty? The pack's future leader? His friend? It was the last thing Zack wanted. But when he considered his choices, he came up empty. He couldn't step aside and surrender Rae to Ty, and he would never convince the old alpha that love should preside over an advantageous match. A huntress mated to the pack alpha would strengthen the old man's bloodline with powerful offspring.

But Jesus, did the thought make him sick.

The air shifted, carrying a whisper from far, far away. *You are a powerful alpha, too. The pack would still benefit.*

If Zack stood a little straighter at the thought, it did him no good. The old alpha had been waiting for an excuse to get rid of Zack for years. He would never back down now.

Ty could be reasoned with, except he was a dutiful son who would never, ever cross his father. That was his sole weakness; it always had been.

"She's mine," Zack repeated, meeting the old man's brutal gaze.

"She's his!" Old Tyrone said, reaching out for his favorite spot on the back of Zack's neck.

Zack smacked the old man's hand away, and the room went deathly quiet. "She's mine."

"A fight, then." Tyrone all but rubbed his hands together in glee. He might not have orchestrated this turn of events, but he certainly would capitalize on them. "To the death!"

Zack saw Ty's eyes slide shut. He wanted a fight as little as Zack did. But what choice did he have?

"Uh..." Cody's voice had all heads turning in his direction. "What about her?" He jabbed a thumb at the door that Rae had fled through.

The old alpha huffed. "Let her run. We don't need a tracker to catch her."

"Catch her?" The mercury in Zack's internal thermometer pushed at the limits of his self-restraint.

"She should have a choice," Tina protested.

"She made her choice when she came here!" Tyrone's bellowed, and the room went still.

Still but for the whisper in Zack's head. *She would have chosen you, if you hadn't fucked this up.*

He pulled his hand away from Ty's chest. "A fight, then."

Ty's eyes locked on his. "A fight."

The old alpha snickered behind them, as always, grabbing the final word. "To the death."

Chapter Nineteen

Images and words hammered in Rae's mind as she ran for the hills. Somehow, she had to escape.

Mate?

Ty?

Tonight?

Old Tyrone had been serious. Worse, he expected her to be grateful. If she hadn't been running full tilt, she would have kicked the ground.

Sabrina, the spoiled daughter of the Westend alpha, was the type to be grateful. Sabrina would do anything for power, just as her father Roric would do. She would even agree to a strategic match, as long as it came with prestige.

Rae stumbled as realization set in. She hadn't been careful enough in Nevada. Someone must have discovered what she was doing on her solitary nocturnal jaunts and deduced who she was, then sold the information to Roric. He, in turn, had sold her to Twin Moon pack.

Who knew her secret? The faces of possible culprits jumped through Rae's mind and only one stuck. The alpha female at Westend was a distant relative of Rae's father. Could she have known what line he had mated into?

More importantly, why? And how did Westend pack stand to benefit?

Her mind spun through the possibilities. Maybe Roric was making a sick trade of some kind, offering her in exchange for a powerful male to come to Westend and mate with Sabrina. The alpha pair had no sons, so Westend pack would need a new alpha someday. A powerful Twin Moon male mated to

Sabrina would keep Roric's bloodline in power and the two packs united.

It made sense, in a warped, medieval way.

But which powerful male from Twin Moon would transfer to Nevada? Ty was destined to lead his home pack, and Zack would be deemed unacceptable. No one else matched the power of those two. Cody might, if he ever stopped playing Peter Pan, the boy who never grew up.

Rae ran on, anger fueling her step. She hated alphas! Alphas and their power plays, manipulating individuals like pawns in a chess game. They were all the same.

And Zack was no better. He'd tricked her. Betrayed her trust. He'd had his fun with her, and then delivered her straight to her doom.

She saw it all in slow motion: Zack naked and hunched over her. God, she'd let him touch—taste!—her everywhere. She'd been thinking *mate* and *forever*, while he'd taken advantage of easy pickings for one hot night. Then he'd handed her over to his own friend as an arranged mate. Maybe they even had some sick sharing arrangement in mind, those two.

Tricked. Betrayed.

Any fool could have seen it coming. But no, she'd done it again—let her imagination take over and fill in one too many blanks. Zack didn't love her. Zack didn't understand her.

And Ty was no better. She thought he was a decent man, but obviously she'd misjudged him. What kind of man would take an arranged mate who didn't want him?

A power-hungry man. One who would force her to submit.

She ran faster, squinting in the dim evening light.

She didn't have it in her to be a ruling alpha's mate. Couldn't they see that? She was born to hunt. And she could never love Ty. Not when her heart was already with Zack.

Her broken heart, she corrected herself. The one that would despise him forever. He'd even had the nerve to tell her, hand on heart, *I will never be like him*, meaning the manipulative old alpha. And she'd believed him.

She ran and ran and ran—in human form because her wolf refused to come out and aid her escape. At the same time, she tried to form some kind of getaway plan. Maybe she could get to her car and get it running. Or hitchhike. Maybe she could head back East and find an enlightened pack to grant her shelter if the Twin Moon wolves came looking.

The East? What would we do there? her wolf protested. *Hunt raccoons? There's no space! Not like here.*

She shoved the beast away. She would go where freedom beckoned, and if that meant the East Coast, so be it. She ran on, begging her wolf to come out and give her twice the speed. Her knowledge of Twin Moon territory was enough to know there were plenty of twists and curves on the northeast edge for her to step off ranch property soon enough.

Just another couple of miles. She gritted her teeth and ran on along a rough track. *Just a little farther...*

She pounded up a punishing slope and paused at the crest of a mesa. The ranch lay behind her, aglow with soft tungsten light. There was a brighter smudge where the dining hall would be, and dots surrounding it where common buildings gave way to a scattering of private homes. It always looked so welcoming at night. Even now, the deceiving effect tried to sway her resolve. But she knew better now. One of those lights came from the council house, where the old alpha had so casually announced her fate.

Where was he now? Where were the others? She watched the headlights of a single truck speed out the ranch gate, kicking up a plume of dust. It was only a question of time before they caught up with her. There would be trucks, wolves—and hell, maybe even Zack on his motorcycle, leading the chase.

She ran downslope in great leaping strides, making for the line of lights on the highway, a few miles distant. Everything hinged on her getting there. Everything.

She had just readjusted her stride to the flatter valley floor when she heard the sharp pant of wolves in pursuit.

Come out and help, you stupid wolf! she yelled at her animal side. Why did it refuse?

A shadow flickered to her left. The wolves were closing in. She could have screamed at the irony. She should be the hunter, not the hunted. Especially when the wolves chasing her were not out to let simply let Mother Earth whisper in her ear.

Her lungs and legs burned with effort, and every muscle straining as she sprinted away.

An excited yip sounded from her right, answered by another immediately behind. The wolves were closing in.

She leaped over a rock and made a clean landing, but her next step found a rut, and her ankle twisted. She tumbled and bottomed out so hard, her vision lit up with a hundred points of light. By the time she scrambled to her knees, the wolves had her surrounded.

Five of them, big, dark, and awfully pleased with themselves, judging by the way their tongues swished over their fangs. Rae did her best to look menacing as she pulled herself to her feet—and promptly lurched as sparks of pain shot through her ankle.

"I am not going back!" she shouted, wondering which wolf was which. None had the smoky scent of the old alpha, but she doubted he would have joined the hunt personally. None had the brownish-black hair of Ty, nor the blond pelt of his brother, Cody.

And none was Zack. She would have spotted her lover from a mile away.

A wolf stepped forward, but a bigger one grunted, sending the first scuttling back to the ranks. Which meant that the big one with the dull brown coat was the highest ranking of the lot.

"I am not going back to Twin Moon Ranch!" she shouted, forcing herself to stand tall.

The wolf's lips curled up before he stepped forward and shifted to human form. She let out a gasp of recognition even before he spoke.

"I don't want you back on Twin Moon, Sunshine. I want you to come with me."

Chapter Twenty

The sun was setting, and instinct urged Zack to follow Rae—north, where his inner compass was pointing most vehemently. But he walked west instead, taking jerky, mechanical steps.

He was off to a fight to the death with his closest friend, for a woman only one of them truly wanted.

He wanted to shake Ty, not that that would do any good. Ty's father's word was his command, and Ty had long since shut down the feeling part of his heart. Zack could practically hear him thinking things through. *Might as well make a match that profits the pack.*

It was wrong, even if Zack knew his best friend would treat Rae right.

We'll fight to the death before giving her up, his coyote and wolf snarled as one.

He could have shaken his head and said, *Yes, it will be death.* The outcome of this fight was a foregone conclusion. He was going to die.

Oh, he could take on Ty, all right. That would make a close fight between two evenly matched wolves. Where Ty had the upper hand in sheer intensity, Zack's agility put him a nose ahead. He might even be able to work around Ty's ultimate weapon: that powerful glare that had melted many a potential opponent. Having play-wrestled Ty since he was a cub, Zack knew how to avoid those eyes.

On a good day, he would give himself a fair chance of holding his own with Ty. Hell, he might even beat the alpha's son. But no matter how well he fought, he'd never come out on top, because Ty had a secret weapon that Zack would always lack.

Family.

Everyone gathered to witness the fight knew that the minute Zack gained the upper hand, the old alpha would jump in and straighten things out.

Zack could take the old man on, easy. Would even enjoy it. He could take Ty on, though he didn't want to. But taking them both on? Maybe even three, what with Ty's brother Cody waiting to pitch in? Never.

The crazy thing was, Ty and Cody were good, honest men. But blood called to blood, and their father would do whatever it took to keep his offspring on top.

Zack ducked between the second and third poles of a fence, heading for the hollow between the old machine shop and a toolshed that was already flooded with artificial light. The place had seen its share of deadly fights back when Tyrone was rising to power, but it hadn't hosted any action for decades now. Zack squinted against the lights, swallowing his bitterness. It hadn't taken the old coot more than five minutes to turn this fight into an event. And Zack, of course, was being ushered to the less favorable side of the ring, where the lights blazed directly into his eyes.

He tried drowning out the noise of the gathering crowd. Old Tyrone was front and center, hammering him with a blazing glare. Ty's siblings were there, too: his raven-haired sister, Tina, and couldn't-be-more-opposite brother, Cody. They stood a conspicuously long step away from their father, eyes cast down to avoid the ugly truth. The nervous knot of Tina's fingers told him that their futures were as closely tied to this fight as Ty's. Today, Ty's mate would be forced on him; tomorrow, it might be Tina. And as for Cody, well, even the swinging bachelor couldn't be far behind.

Family. Ty had his back to a mountain; Zack had his to an abyss.

"Get him!" Tyrone barked at his son.

Zack saw Ty's eyes tighten in a wince. Family had its pluses and minuses.

Making no move to start, he waited for Ty. This fight wasn't about winning; it was about buying Rae time to escape, hopefully to a pack where the alpha let her choose her own mate.

He swallowed the thought like a bitter pill. Rae with another man? She was his, and he was hers. They were destined for each other.

Except destiny had its hiccups, just like life. He took in the scene around him—Ty's clenched fists, the old alpha's narrowed eyes, the spectators behind him—and knew it was not to be. He and Rae had already had all the time fate had allotted them.

God, it hurt to consider that. And the way she'd looked at him with accusing eyes—that was even worse. Even if he won this impossible fight, Rae would never take him back.

Ty stepped forward, looking darker and more haunted than ever. Zack circled, trying for a better angle against the glare—and not much else. He had to drag this out, which meant fighting long and hard, and possibly wounding Ty enough to keep him from pursuing Rae. The thought sickened him. Why was he even fighting his friend?

For Rae, his wolf snarled as Ty unleashed his first blow.

Half the crowd went into a frenzy. The other half hushed as Zack ducked and swung back, landing a glancing blow off Ty's shoulder.

"Come on, Ty!" a shrill voice cried. Audrey, the ranch playgirl, knew how to side with the winning team.

They shuffled around each other, knuckles raised, chins low, looking for an opening. Ty came in with a bolo punch then followed up with a series of lackluster jabs Zack could parry with ease. The vocal part of the crowd cheered in excitement. Old Tyrone, of course, was barking for blood.

"Get him!"

"Why don't they shift?" someone in the crowd cried.

Zack knew as well as Ty why not. Fighting with their fists kept the damage to a minimum. Neither one of them had his heart in this fight. Anyone could see it in the way they traded blows any quick-witted kid could have avoided.

Ty advanced with a quick combination that Zack had perfectly under control until his footwork brought him in a direct line with old Tyrone's sights. The man's laser-like glare distracted him long enough to let Ty land a punch on his chin. Zack stumbled back, and a gasp went out from the crowd.

"Follow up, follow up!" Old Tyrone yelled.

Ty lumbered slowly forward, giving Zack ample time to get his bearings before he came in with an easy uppercut. Zack smacked it away and followed with a very wide hook.

That's when he saw it: the wrinkle in the corner of Ty's mouth. Not quite a smile, but a smile all the same.

He's doing it, too. Ty was pulling his punches, throwing pitty-pat blows that wouldn't hurt a kid. Because Rae's escape, he realized, suited Ty, too.

He hid a smile and went back at Ty with a haymaker guaranteed to go wide.

Perfect, his coyote snickered, trying to make the punch look good.

Perfect except for one thing, as he realized when the fight wore on. It was impossible to put two alpha wolves in one ring and expect them to play nice. Bit by bit, he felt his wolf creeping toward the surface, in the same way that Ty's eyes grew more intent. So much that Zack took to avoiding them altogether, just in case. With every blow, every parry, every grunt from the audience, the fight escalated.

Showtime was over. Soon, he would be fighting for his life. Rae's life, too. She would die before giving in to a forced mate.

Ty's blows came faster and in more effective combinations. Eyes stinging with the salt of his own sweat, Zack did his best to leash his inner beast. But Ty came at him harder and harder, and Zack was forced to put more power behind his own punches. When Ty got in a good uppercut, Zack responded with a heavy cross that pulled a vicious growl out of Ty. Zack stepped left, looking for an opening, while Ty went right, his shoulders blocking the floodlights. But then Ty slid farther, and a beam of light pierced Zack's eyes. He threw a hand up against it, blotting out the blinding combination of floodlights and the old alpha's glare.

There was a mighty crack, and Zack had the vague feeling it might have been his jaw. At least, that's as much as his mind registered as he flew sprawling across the hard-packed dirt. When he could process something other than the pain shooting through his jaw, it was an inky sky with tiny points of lights, soothing and soft.

Beautiful. Like jewels in the sky.

He focused there, trying to blink away the pain. A hulking form shifted into view above him: Ty, leaning in to assess the impact of that last blow.

The word echoed in Zack's mind, bringing out a crazy smile. There'd been an impact, all right. Rae. The woman had been like a meteor in his life, rocketing in and changing everything.

He could have howled, thinking of her gone, but in that off-balance moment, his coyote got the better of him and started laughing. His gurgling chuckle turned into a throaty laugh that built until his jaw and ribs ached.

He flopped back into the warm earth and took in the scene around him, feeling strangely removed from it all. The lights, the barn, his packmates. A tiny and strangely absurd universe. Ty frowned, and his eyes went from killer to confused.

What the hell is so funny? Ty's voice thundered in his mind.

Try two friends fighting over a woman one of them doesn't want and the other one wants too much.

Zack laughed until tears blurred his sight. The bubbling laughter grew louder and deeper, as if a bass drum had just seen the humor in this strange scene and decided to rumble along. When he paused to suck in a breath, the sound went on, and he realized it was Ty, leaning over with his hands on his knees, either from a laughter-induced shake or the exhaustion of the fight. Maybe a little of both.

A soft, scolding voice from the past echoed in his ears: old Aunt Jean, the former schoolteacher and surrogate mother to underdogs like him. What would she say to them now?

Two little ragamuffins, laughing in the dirt.

The recollection only made Zack laugh harder. They couldn't have been more than eight when she said it, that day on the schoolhouse grounds. And that had to have been the first and last time anyone had associated the word *muffin* with him or Ty.

He laughed until Ty reached a hand down to haul him to his feet—whether to restart the fight or dust his ass off and head for a bar, Zack wasn't sure. He gripped the rough hand as if to stand, but then yanked Ty down beside him. There was a heavy moment of silence before their laughter picked up where it had left off, and for a minute, they really were a couple of ragamuffins in the dirt.

They spent a few minutes like that, the two of them, while their mute packmates looked on, unsure how to react. Then Zack took a deep breath and threw an arm out to tap Ty.

"Oof," the alpha's son let out, biting back a grimace. "That rib's broken, man."

Zack rolled to all fours, slowly, painfully, then sat back on his haunches and gingerly touched his chin. "So's my fucking jaw."

"How broken?" Ty challenged, and Zack grinned. It was another line from the past, one they'd used back in their play-fight days.

Except this was no play-fight. This was real, and Rae was out there. He locked eyes with Ty, suddenly going quiet.

Rae. Mate, his wolf growled. *Mine.*

Ty's eyes flared, and Zack wondered how this night might end. Would their friendship be forever ruined or renewed?

A slow second later, Ty gave a curt nod and accepted Zack's hand up.

"What the hell is this?" Old Tyrone barked.

Zack stiffened, but Ty jerked his hand northeast, in the direction Rae had gone.

"Got a mate to catch," Ty declared in a quiet but deadly voice. "*His* mate," he added, jabbing his chin toward Zack.

A moment later, they were both in wolf form, sprinting into the night.

Chapter Twenty-One

Much as Rae blinked, she couldn't change the reality confronting her. Jed was back. And this time, with reinforcements: four strapping young wolves who looked hungry for action—any kind of action they could get.

"Sunshine, you knew I wouldn't let that jackass take you away. Now, come home with me." Jed's voice went from sugar sweet to acid sharp on the final words.

Home? She leaned toward the ranch, then forced herself ramrod straight. There was no home for her. Not with Jed, not with Zack, not with any man. She nearly barked it out but held her tongue, not wanting to set Jed off.

He was crazy. She could see it in his eyes. Crazy and utterly convinced of himself—a dangerous combination. Forget about reasoning with him. So what if she wasn't interested in him and never had been? So what if she had her own dream? That was all negligible in the madman's master plan. Jed wanted a mate, a pack, and supreme rule. And he would stop at nothing to get it.

"Sunshine, you okay?" His eyes shone in the dark. "I should never have let that asshole take you away. But I wasn't ready to take on the whole pack, so I had to let you go. For your own sake. But you see?" He broke out in a proud grin, waiting for her approval. "I came back for you, just like I promised."

Her stomach twisted and rolled. He'd promised, all right.

Jed would never stop coming after her. He would never give up. Coming from another man, that might have been touching. With Jed, it was terrifying.

Instinct told her to flee, a plan her wolf was all on board with.

Let me out! Let me run!

Although she'd been wishing for her wolf's help, she reined the urge in. Running would only set off the chase instinct in these wolves. From the looks of it, Jed had assembled a gang of young males cast out from their home packs. They would have been kicked out when they were still immature and manageable. Now, though, they had filled out—like Jed— becoming formidable fighting machines. Jed's vision of taking over Colorado's North Ridge pack might be less suicidal than it first seemed. She could see it now: Jed had probably promised each of these vigilantes leading roles in his new pack if they helped him overthrow Greer, the pack alpha. Even for rogues, the call of a pack was strong.

So was the call of the chase. If she ran, they would follow, bring her down, and... She didn't want to think about the rest.

Jed, though, seemed excited about exactly that. "Hey, Sunshine. Why don't we play? You run, we chase." The wolf to Jed's left licked his chops, and Jed grinned. "Where I come from, brother, we share our prizes. She's mine, but if you're good, you can have a taste, too."

Rae's stomach folded in on itself. Jed had learned one trick too many from Greer, that greedy brute. Neither of them was half the man Zack was.

Then she cursed herself. Why did Zack pop back into her mind? She had banished the thought of him. Or tried to, anyway. Zack had betrayed her. He was as bad as the rest.

She could only count on herself. So, how was she going to get out of this mess?

Run, the wolf said.

She tested her ankle, finding the pain gone. Either it was only a twist, or her accelerated shifter healing had already gone to work. The ankle would hold if she ran.

Fight, her heart cried.

Talk, logic urged.

"Look, Jed, we need to think this through. Are you really going to take on Greer with four wolves?"

He grinned, his teeth flashing white in the night. "Who says I only got four?"

Her heart sank as three more wolves slunk out of the shadows. Seven wolves—eight, with Jed.

Despair seeped into her shoulders, and she wondered if she should give in and hope Jed took it easy on her. Maybe later, she would get some chance to escape.

"I know, I know," Jed crowed. "You're impressed. Old Jed is finally moving up in the world. And you, Sunshine, are climbing right along with me. So, get moving! We got our trucks parked a couple of miles away."

"Right, climbing," she murmured.

More like descending the steps to hell. Her mind spun, looking for some way out. The minute she let these wolves close ranks around her, her chances of escape were nil. It was eight to one, with more arriving any time because the Twin Moon wolves were after her too. Soon.

Her heart jumped on the idea. How soon?

The Twin Moon wolves would fight these rogues off, which would suit her just fine. But then what?

Before she had the chance to think out a plan, her wolf tore out of her skin and started to run in the direction of the ranch.

In an instant, they were after her—eight baying wolves already lost in the thrill of the chase. She could make out Jed's scratchy tenor among the others. He sounded delighted with his mate's cooperation in a bit of fun.

Well, she didn't want any part of it. Her legs pounded the dirt as her eyes picked out the best path through the scrub ahead. Jed and his gang were running for sport, but she was running for her life, and that kept her three lengths ahead.

For now, at least. She hammered up the slope she'd come flying down earlier. It was hard going over loose scree and rocks, but she made the most of her lead, kicking back all the loose material she could to hinder those in pursuit. One wolf, though, was making steady progress up a parallel route and slowly closing in. The crazed gleam in his eyes and curled lips identified it as Jed in wolf form. His claws scuttled over rock as he launched himself in her direction. It was only a burst of speed, together with lucky footing, that allowed her to jump clear.

Whoosh! His outstretched paws swept the air an inches behind her.

Jed cursed into her mind as he fell back into the rhythm of running.

Rae's muscles wailed with each desperate step she heaved up the final yards of the slope.

Close—so close!

The flat edge of the mesa was right there. Once she reached it, she would gain precious seconds if freewheeled down the other side before Jed followed. And after that?

Damned if she knew.

Forcing her screaming muscles to obey, she threw herself over the rise—and immediately dove out of the way of two wolves hurtling up from the opposite direction. One was blackish-brown, darker than night. The other, a familiar deep brown.

Zack. A wave of relief came over her even as she tumbled. Zack would help.

Her body ground to a halt against a boulder, but the impact hurt less than the thought that followed.

Zack had betrayed her. She could never trust him again.

Behind her, the wolves crashed together, and the night exploded with sound. She had never heard roars so fierce and outraged, not even back in Colorado, where fights were a regular occurrence.

Run! Instinct screamed in Rae's ear as she rolled to her feet. *Let them fight while we get away.*

Three shaky steps later, she petered to a stop.

Zack and Ty had come for her. She couldn't run and leave them to fight her fight, could she?

On the other hand, they hadn't really come to help. They had only come to claim her for their pack. Whichever side won the skirmish splitting the night behind her, it would all be the same in the end. She would be nothing more than the spoil of war.

Zack is not the same! her wolf insisted, shuffling around so that she faced the fight.

One trembling step after another, she crept toward the action at the crest of the hill, fighting herself every inch of the way.

Zack and the other wolf—it had to be Ty, given his coloring and the intensity of his glare—were firmly planted on a stage-like rise of the mesa, taking lethal swipes at the wolves attacking them. The two of them were an army to themselves, so big and angry that the air around them wavered. One of Jed's gang was already down while another dragged himself out of the melee. The others jumped in and out of range. Zack roared in an outraged tone that she would never have imagined coming from him. He batted away an attacking wolf with one broad paw and followed up with jaws that flashed white.

The next time they flashed, they were red. Rae gulped. Three down, five to go. Could Zack and Ty do it?

Her eyes swept over the battlefield and counted again. Four—she could only find four other wolves. Where was the other?

The air pressure by her left ear squeezed and shook, and she spun to find Jed, leaping in to force her back against a boulder. He'd snuck around the others and cut in around the rear.

Come on, Sunshine. He smiled. *Let's go.*

Even at the height of the fight, the man was grinning. She could feel him forcing his words into her mind.

You and me, Sunshine. Just like old times.

Chapter Twenty-Two

Rae stepped back. *There were no old times.*

Jed's growl became a snarl. *Come now, Sunshine.*

I will never come with you!

With one angry swipe, her claws ripped his shoulder, opening four parallel gashes just deep enough to stoke his anger.

The growl turned low and deadly as Jed faced her, his tail slashing the air like a saber. *You are mine.*

He lunged for her, and she sprang away, scrambling to a landing. Jed paused, wild-eyed and bristling as she bared her fangs.

I love it when women play with me, he chuckled.

She wondered how many women had suffered at his hands. How much pain would he inflict on her if he won? The fact that Jed wouldn't kill her was a small consolation.

You have a twisted definition of play, she growled, backing toward a boulder. She needed some point of orientation in this crazy night. Jed stood before her and at least another half-dozen wolves battled just out of sight at her back.

You are sick. She all but spat the words out.

His grin bent into a frown. *And you are mine.*

I will never be yours!

She'd barely formed the words when he leaped. Dodging at the last minute, she hoped he would crash into the rock. But Jed twisted and roared, catching her haunches in his front paws. His claws scraped along her ribs, trying to get a grip.

All mine, Sunshine, he growled. The threat drummed from her ears to her desperately calculating mind.

She wanted to scream for a miracle burst of adrenaline to heave the brute away. She tried dragging herself free, but Jed was too heavy. With a push and a grunt, he worked himself higher, shouldering her into a roll. An instant later, he had her pinned and clacked his ivory fangs in her face.

All I have to do is bite, bitch, and you will finally understand that you are mine.

He lowered his muzzle, going for her neck. She could feel the sappy drip of saliva work its way through her ruff even before his teeth scraped along her skin. Either he'd gut her there and then, or bite clean and deep in a mating bite that would bind her permanently to him. Either way, there would be no escape.

She wanted to squeeze her eyes shut and pretend the horror of it away, but she forced herself to act. Even death would be better than a lifetime of abuse. With a mighty kick, she raked the claws of her back leg along his belly, drawing blood.

Bitch!

Jed pulled back to study the wound. When he looked up again, his eyes were sheer malice, and she knew it was the end. She opened her jaws in defense when he came back at her, but she knew she couldn't win. He slammed her back onto the earth, knocking the wind out of her lungs, and took up position over her throat.

Mine! His hot breath burned her skin.

Rae writhed in a last act of defense before the inevitable bite. Behind Jed's looming body were the stars. So beautiful, so far away. She closed her eyes.

There was an explosion of sound, a tussle, and suddenly, Jed's weight was lifted away. Instinct brought Rae to her feet, and she would have fled if she hadn't been disoriented by the eruption of sound and shape before her.

Jed and another wolf were wrestling on the south side of the ridge, just steps away from her. His opponent was a mighty wolf with a satchel-brown, dun-tinted coat. Half coyote, half wolf.

Zack. Rae knew her heart was foolish to swell at the sight of him, but it did anyway.

Jed launched a counterattack, howling his rage, and there was the sickening rip of flesh as Zack staggered. A moment later, he battled back in a burst of energy that drove Jed to his haunches. The wolves scrambled for each other's throats, boxing and slashing until they broke apart, then crashed together again.

It was a fight of finesse and calculated blows versus raw power, each wolf briefly gaining the upper hand before the other wrestled it away. Jed rolled, using his greater weight to take Zack with him, and Rae let out a scream. *No!*

Zack's face lit briefly before folding into a snarl, and he pushed Jed back with strength he shouldn't have possessed. Then he was on top of Jed, jaws held wide.

It was over in a splash of crimson and a garbled cry. Rae swayed on her feet, not sure if it was relief or fear that was pounding through her veins. Jed was dead.

That moment was her chance at escape, but she found herself rooted to the spot, eyes closed, waiting.

Waiting for what? part of her mind screamed.

She forced her eyes open at the sound of footsteps and a growl. Zack's power preceded him like a battering ram, and she found herself flopping belly-up in submission. A moment later, he was hovering over her throat, just as Jed had, with his clover green eyes wide and hungry.

Zack's scent hit her, and for a moment, she saw everything that could have been. A home. A future. A good life with a good man.

A betrayal.

She closed her eyes, wishing the past three weeks away. There was a time when she'd trusted the man inside that wolf, even wanted him. And dammit, part of her still wanted Zack. But she would never submit to being claimed against her will.

Every muscle in her tensed as she twisted her head away, gasping for one final breath of freedom. Zack's breath heated her neck, and behind him, the darkness of the night pressed in.

Ten seconds passed, and then ten more, and still neither of them moved. She was vaguely aware that the fight between the other wolves and Ty had settled into ponderous silence, but that barely mattered now. She kept her eyes shut tightly, waiting for the end.

But it was a gentle hand, not pointed fangs, that ran over her throat. A human hand that traced a light line along her neck. She blinked and found that Zack had shifted. Somehow, he'd taken her with him, because her wolf had slipped away, leaving the woman pinned under the man. A man hanging his head so low, his hair brushed her chest. She froze, trying not to breathe.

Zack made a choked sound then slowly backed off her and lurched to his feet, heaving her up with one hand.

She swayed. Zack's face was a mess of blood and indecision. When he reached out for her, she jumped out of reach.

Shame shadowed his face. *I didn't want any of this to happen. I only wanted you.*

Rae didn't know if she'd read the words in his face or in his mind, but there they were.

I only wanted you.

Her eyes stung with tears she refused to set free. The two of them might have remained standing there all night like two sad statues had an engine not sounded in the distance. Ty came over the ridge, still in wolf form and red around the muzzle. His ears pointed toward the sound. Behind him, all was silent, telling Rae Jed's rogues were vanquished.

The wolves threatening to steal her soul were gone, only to be replaced by two others who threatened the same thing—and a rapidly approaching third. Would it be the old alpha? Would Ty claim her now? Or would he drag her back to the ranch and force himself upon her right there?

A motorcycle roared up: Zack's Harley, with another man in the seat. It was Cody, Ty's younger brother, looking uncharacteristically grim.

He nodded to Rae in a curt greeting then quickly yanked his eyes from her naked body to Zack. The four of them stood there in silence even after Ty blurred back to his human form.

She waited. Surely Ty would make some proclamation now. After all, he was the pack's future alpha.

But it was Zack who moved first, stepping to the motorcycle and pulling the key from the ignition. The warrior in him was back; she could see it in the square of his shoulders, the clench of his jaw. But he was a weary warrior who'd lost sight of his cause. With a grunt and a jerk of the chin, he ordered the other men to back away.

To her utter surprise, Ty and Cody only hesitated briefly before complying. For that moment, at least, they ceded rank to their packmate.

When Zack faced her, his face was limp in defeat even though he stood on the scene of a triumph. He mimicked a toss then threw Rae the key. It came arcing to her in slow motion, as if the world was decelerating on its axis to give her a chance to think.

Zack was giving her his bike.

Zack was giving her her freedom.

Zack was letting her go.

She reached out and fisted the key in one hand. Freedom. Her emotions swung somewhere between elation and grief.

Zack leaned over the bike and pulled something from the saddlebag then laid it across the seat. He stepped aside, holding his hands up as if she had a gun pointed his way.

"You're letting me go? Why?" Her voice had never sounded so raspy and unsure.

His lips moved, though no sound came out. It was his eyes that said it. *Because I love you.*

A memory said the rest. *You know, that corny line. If you love something, set it free.*

She looked out beyond the desert to the pulsing lights of the highway. She was free to go anywhere she wanted, to forge her own way.

Her heart thumped. The only place she wanted to be was here, with him.

Then she gave herself a stubborn shake and remembered: she was supposed to head far, far away. East—that had been her plan. The outside world and her future, lay just over there, where headlights were streaking by. Meanwhile, Zack stood nearby, watching her as if she had her finger on a grenade.

With a gulp, Rae made her decision. So what if it made her miserable for the rest of her life? Snatching the flannel shirt Zack had laid out on the motorcycle, she buttoned it hastily over her torso. It smelled just like him, dammit, fresh and musky and true, as if all the power and the harsh beauty of the desert had been woven into the fibers. The shirt was just long enough that she wouldn't be arrested for indecent exposure once she got on the highway and made her escape. From there—well, she'd wing it.

With every muscle screaming in protest, she threw a leg over the motorcycle, kicked the engine to life, and roared off, forcing herself to look forward, not back.

No looking back, she ordered herself. *Too late now.*

Rae. Zack's whisper carried on the wind, half plea and all heart.

She gunned the engine and rode on, tears streaming down her face.

Chapter Twenty-Three

Zack forced himself to watch his mate speed down the bumpy trail and across the flats, the sound of a receding engine all too familiar to his ears. He stood long and utterly silent, following the single light until it paused on the edge of the highway, then merged and was swallowed up by the rest.

Gone. Rae was gone.

This is where his sense of honor got him: on the wrong end of a dust cloud, with his destined mate speeding out of his life. He vaguely registered a faint sound and wondered if it was his heart shattering, muted by the flesh and fibers in between.

Well, let it. He didn't need that particular organ any more.

He stood there a long time after Ty and Cody left, staring into emptiness. Then he walked back to the ranch, his step as slow as it had been fast and frantic on the way out. There was nothing to run back to. Just an empty cabin, his packmates, and an angry alpha. Not that the latter bothered him much. The fight against Ty had been a draw, but the confrontation with old Tyrone had been a clear win.

Respect. He'd won that, even if it was a small consolation for losing his mate. But life was what it was: cruel. Twisted. Unfair. He climbed the stairs to his porch and settled into his chair, feeling a thousand years older and none too wiser. Just emptier inside.

The aches in his body faded gradually, all but the one that mattered most.

∞∞∞

Over the next two weeks, Zack fell back into his usual routine: doing odd jobs on the ranch by day, sitting on his porch at night, watching the stars arc slowly across the sky. Wondering if Rae was watching them too. The fact that there'd been a dearth of tracking assignments was just fine with him, because heading out to track would remind him too much of that magical night they had shared.

Spring was coming, even in the absence of Rae's scent. Paintbrush erupted in startling orange-red. Desert marigolds waved from the ends of their stalks. Hummingbirds zipped merrily to and fro. But scenes that should have sung with promise and new beginnings only cried regret in his ears.

Days stumbled along, and nights dragged, over and over, right up to the night of the new moon. Rae would be out hunting, he figured, a swift shadow in the night. She was out there somewhere. He sat, hushed, wondering if he'd hear Mother Earth's whisper if he tried hard enough.

He strained his ears until most of the night was gone, dreaming of his bike, the open road, and two tight arms around his waist. He dreamed it so desperately that when his chin fell on his chest, jerking him awake, the sound of a motorcycle engine still rumbled in his ears.

He creaked to his feet and turned for the screen door, resigning himself to another sleepless night. Then he paused at the threshold, because the engine noise was still there. Growing steadily louder, in fact, until he heard 750 familiar cc's come up the drive. He braced both hands against the doorframe and tucked his chin, keeping his back to the road. If this was his imagination coming to torture him again, he wasn't going to play along.

The engine purred right up to the porch and stood humming quietly for half a minute before the driver shut it off. Then it was only the crickets, the night owl, and his desperately fragile hope, dangling in the desert air.

Chapter Twenty-Four

Rae's legs were shaky as she climbed the steps to Zack's cabin, and it wasn't due to the miles in her weary bones. The past weeks were a blur now: the mountains, the truck stops, the tears. Every bump in every mile of road had rattled through the handlebars, into her arms, and through her body until her teeth ached as much as her shoulders or back.

None of it held a candle to the ache in her heart, though, so she had driven on and on out of sheer determination—or stubborn stupidity. She'd driven past the barrens of Texas, past an ocean of bluegrass in Tennessee, and on to the tidewaters of Maryland until she saw the sun rise over the ocean. She'd nearly driven off the end of the rickety dock she'd stopped on, not caring what kind of end she'd meet. Because all those miles had taught her one thing: that the world was just as bleak and twice as lonely as it had been back in the desert.

She had checked in to a cheap motel and fell into a forty-eight-hour delirium of sleep, figuring it would do her good. But crawling out the other side of that tunnel was even harder, because where was the light?

There was no light, not without him.

She hated herself for even thinking it. She was supposed to be independent and strong, dammit. And Zack had set her up only to let her take a mighty fall.

Or had he?

He saved us, her wolf insisted. *He loves us.*

Love or lust? Do alphas even know the difference?

Her wolf growled. *This one does. He fought for us.*

She tried ignoring the flutter in her stomach. *He fought so he could claim us. Make us his. Take our freedom.*

The wolf raged at the suggestion. *He let us go. He gave us this thing you call freedom. And what good is it?*

Freedom is everything.

Freedom is alone.

Rae bowed her head to the truth. She didn't like this new situation any better than her inner wolf did. But sooner or later, she told herself, she'd find a new pack. The right pack.

Her wolf whined. *We found the right pack back at Twin Moon Ranch.*

She pictured the high-altitude desert of central Arizona. The vast landscape—harsh yet beautiful at the same time. The tidy settlement, the friendly faces, and the meandering path to the cabin on the periphery. That's where her thoughts led every time she let them wander. To a cabin, a porch, and a man.

An honest man, or a liar?

There was a fine line between trust and treason, that was for sure. But beyond that? She didn't know whether to believe her mind or her heart.

She had considered the question for two pensive weeks, wandering to the shoreline each night, trying to find some shimmer of truth in the moonlight rippling over the waves. She'd tossed pebbles into the water and listened for the splashes. It wouldn't be long before the next new moon, and then where would she be?

A shadow flitted overhead—an osprey soaring effortlessly. Wings outstretched, it leaned into a wide turn and circled around, honing in on its prey. Rae watched, glad to distract herself from her thoughts. The osprey caught an updraft, soared effortlessly upward, then wheeled. Looking. Waiting. Calculating.

A second shadow joined the first. The osprey's mate? Rae's eyes narrowed and blurred until she didn't see a bird but a wolf, loping along in support of its mate.

Then the memories came back in a flood. The night of the pronghorn hunt had been magic—every moment of it. For the first time in her life, everything had clicked perfectly: the new moon, the prey, the place. The man at her side. Her lips curled into a smile just at the memory of it, but then fell into a frown, remembering what came next.

Joy.

Anger.

Betrayal.

The gutted expression on Zack's face.

For the hundredth time, she replayed the memory of him tossing the keys in slow motion, giving her freedom. Why?

The first osprey dipped and curved, while the second remained watchful, high above.

If you love something, set it free.

There was a second part to that corny old line, she remembered.

If it loves you, it will come back. If it doesn't...

Her heart skipped a beat, and she forced herself to rewind and picture it all over again: the mesa, the motorcycle, the man. One who faced up to his own shortcomings and took his punishment on the chin.

Was she woman enough to do the same?

Because Zack hadn't betrayed her. Old Tyrone's announcement that she was to mate with Ty had hit Zack as hard as it hit her. His gutted expressed had said as much, only she hadn't been paying attention at the time. Zack hadn't suspected what the pack alpha was planning. He wasn't bringing her to mate with someone else. He'd just been bringing her home.

He loved her. And he'd risked everything for her—his life, his honor, his standing in the pack.

And what had she done for him?

Shame flooded her, and a moment later, resolve. Then she was on her feet, scrambling for the bike, fumbling with the key.

Drive slowly, the human part of her mind said. *Be sure.*

Her wolf snarled. *I'm sure. Just get me back to my mate!*

The closer she got, the faster she drove, desperate to fast-forward herself back into his arms. Zack—an imperfect man, but her perfect mate.

Sixty-plus hours and four brief stops later, she crossed the Arizona state line. Even then, it was another couple of hours before she reached the dirt road branching off the highway and to the ranch. As she bumped over it, doubt spread in a heavy layer over her exhaustion. Would she even be allowed back on the ranch? She had defied the alpha and rejected his son. She had turned her back on Zack. Would he even forgive her? Would he want her?

The questions hounded her right up to the moment when she climbed the porch, her legs trembling from more than just road fatigue. But each step made her feel more and more certain, as if destiny was nodding her on.

She stepped to within a breath of Zack's back and stood there, soaking in his scent.

Chapter Twenty-Five

Zack kept his back turned as the driver took a long time getting off that bike, and an even longer time climbing the three creaky steps to his porch. An eternity passed before Rae slipped slowly into his space, like he was a spooked colt liable to bolt at any minute. His skin tingled even before a warm hand eased his fingers open and pressed something thin and edgy inside.

A key. The key to his Harley.

"Thanks for the loan," Rae said. She spoke like she'd just been down the road and back, but he caught the waver in her voice.

He talked toward the doorframe, forcing the words off his clunky tongue. "Planning on getting a new ride?"

The air moved as she shook her head, and the tip of her nose brushed his neck. She was that close, and boy, did that feel good.

"I'm planning on staying put, if I'm allowed."

He exhaled, waiting for his heart to restart. Allowed? He'd make damn sure Rae never wanted to leave.

"Shouldn't you be out hunting?" He tried to sound unaffected, but he could barely breathe.

She nodded into his back and snuck her arms around him just as she'd done on his bike, an eternity ago.

"Different kind of hunt tonight," she whispered.

Th-thump, th-thump. So his heart did work, after all.

"What kind of hunt is that?"

A finger brushed against his cheek. "Man hunt."

His fingers curled around hers. "You think he's going to come willingly?

"I think he can be convinced."

That's when something in him cracked. He spun and pulled her tight, squeezing to make it clear he didn't plan to ever let go.

"I'm sorry I left," Rae croaked from where she was wrapped around his neck. Her arms clenched and reclenched to hug him from a dozen different angles.

He buried his nose in her hair, wondering if anything had ever felt this good. For once, someone was speeding into his life instead of speeding out.

"I'm sorry for everything else."

She shook her head. "No more sorry."

"No more goodbyes."

"No more anything but this," she agreed.

They hung on to each other like a couple of castaways still holding tight hours after being washed ashore. With every inhale, Zack felt stronger, surer. A feeling a man like Ty must have all the time—that he had a mountain at his back, and not an abyss. He had love. More than that, he had pure, unconditional love. Something Ty might never have, for all his unspoken privilege.

"Hey," Rae whispered in his ear. "Listen."

Zack hugged her closer instead of lifting his head, but even wrapped tightly in that spring-scented cloak she seemed to wear, he heard it. A whisper in the air, faint as filtered starlight from a thousand light-years away. A whisper that carried images, not words, forming a scene in his mind.

There was a little cabin, a crackling fireplace, and a bowl of untouched popcorn. A couple of carefree lovers settled back on a thick rug, their legs intertwined. A cabin very much like his, with a fresh paint job, a neat stack of firewood, and a bow leaning against one corner of the porch.

There, the image seemed to be saying. *That is where you must go.*

When Rae's breath caught, he knew she saw it too.

"But we're already here," he murmured.

"There's place," she said, letting her lips stroll over his cheek, "And there's time."

He replayed the winter scene in his mind. Maybe they did need a little time to find their rhythm. With spring just breaking over the desert now, they were three seasons away from letting that scene play out in real time. Plenty of time to settle in together and to finish those projects on the house.

Rae smiled into his cheek, and her thoughts projected into his mind. *Time to hunt.*

To track, he added, with the coyote and wolf nodding along.

To love, Rae finished. *To mate.*

Epilogue

Three months & three new moons later...

Rae sat on the top step of the porch, gazing out over the desert as she waited for her mate to come home.

Home. She breathed it all in, from the tiniest speck of yellow flower to the banded hills that showcased millions of years of Mother Earth's labor. A good place for a hunter, with miles to roam on new moon nights and a ranch to help operate in the weeks in between. All that with a man she could call her mate.

Her heart bubbled as it always did when Zack appeared around the bend, his tall frame silhouetted against the blaze of the setting sun. If only she could see his face. Would it be etched with worry or creased in a smile?

"So, how did it go?" she asked when her mate was three steps away.

He sighed and sat beside her, slinging an arm over her shoulders.

"It went."

She wrapped her hand around his thigh and snuggled in close. His warmth poured into her, as it always did when they touched.

"Well, what did they say?"

Zack snorted. "Doesn't matter what they said. What mattered was what I said."

She could picture it perfectly—her man standing up to the leaders of two packs: old Tyrone of Twin Moon Ranch and Roric of Westend pack, who'd come over from Nevada to sort out what Tyrone called *This mess.*

Would have been nice to see that in person, her wolf grinned.

She shrugged the thought away. Much as she'd tried to work up the nerve to attend the meeting in the council house, she just didn't have it in her. She needed her energy for tonight's hunt, and spending it listening to a couple of old geezers blow steam wouldn't help.

She shivered and tugged Zack's arm tighter around her, thinking how close she'd come to another kind of life. If she had been Ty's mate, she would have been in for a lifetime of meetings, obligations, and compromises. If she had have been forced to be Jed's mate, she would have been in for a lifetime of abuse. Either way, a lifetime of regret.

"Hey," Zack murmured. "You okay?"

She touched her forehead to his shoulder and breathed him in. "Yep. I'm okay."

In truth, she was more than okay. A lifetime of love and hope stretched before her. She took several deep breaths, processing her luck.

"So what did you say?" she finally prompted.

"Well, first Roric ranted about broken contracts, pack alliances, and a lot of other nonsense."

She could picture that. Easily.

"Until I told him you're not a clause in a contract or a puppet in some game," Zack said, his voice rasping just a bit.

Her wolf swelled with pride, all but purring over her fine choice in a mate.

"And what did he do?"

Zack snorted. "He shut up."

Now that, she would have liked to see. "What about old Tyrone?"

He chuckled. "You should have seen Ty stand him down."

"How? What did Ty say?"

Zack threaded his fingers through hers. "He didn't say anything. He just stared and stared until the old man grumbled and looked away."

That glare was easy to picture. A damn good thing she'd never been on the receiving end of it.

"And that was it?"

Zack nodded in satisfaction. "That was it."

She ran her fingers through the hair at the nape of his neck. Her mate had done her proud—again.

"Not like they could do anything about us now," Zack chuckled, fingering the faint mark on her neck.

She tingled at his touch and the hot memories they stirred. That had been quite a night—their first full moon together. They'd run, played, then come back to the cabin and made love until the sun came up.

Oh, much longer than that, her wolf corrected with a lusty growl.

She blushed in spite of herself, remembering some of their antics. Somewhere along the line, round three had gone from warm and sweet to hot and hard. She could still see the glow in Zack's eyes when he went down for the mating bite. She could still feel herself rising to meet it because she knew what kind of possessiveness it would bring. And she could still see the happy glaze in his eyes after she'd reciprocated. They were one now, mated for life.

Zack's mind, though, must have still been on the meeting.

"Ty did good," he murmured.

"You did good. Both of you. It's high time those old alphas had someone stand up to them."

A changing of the guard was long overdue. Someday, change might even come to Greer's brutal regime at North Ridge pack.

In any case, change was coming to Twin Moon Ranch, her new home. With Ty stepping up to the plate and Zack there to support him, the future looked brighter than ever.

A corner of her heart squeezed and sighed. "Do you think Ty will ever find his mate?"

Zack considered the question long enough for Rae to sense his doubt. She'd heard what happened years ago—how Ty had nearly found then lost his mate. Even if his thick hide didn't show it, the scars were there, and she doubted that any of the local girls had it in them to heal those wounds.

"Maybe she'll find him." Zack's whisper carried into the night like a wish.

A wish Rae heartily seconded. All of her own were fulfilled, so it was time others got their due. Especially Ty, who had shown his integrity when it mattered most.

A firefly flitted past, drunk on the serenity of the night. Rae rubbed her palm against Zack's thigh, ready to wrap up the subject and file it away. The past was past, the future was theirs.

"What happened next?"

Zack shrugged. "I told them it was time to hunt, and we left—me and Ty." He leaned in for another kiss. "We can't keep the pack waiting."

Rae smiled against his lips. "How many tonight?"

"Depends if you count Cody. He wants to know if we get to kill anything tonight."

She play-smacked his arm. "Men."

He pulled her into a hug that pinned her arms safely to her sides. "Don't blame all of us."

She melted into his body in spite of herself, and then jerked her mind back to the hunt. Business first.

Followed by pleasure, her wolf added.

Yes, there'd be that, too. Guaranteed.

"So how many?" she asked, trying to get back on track.

Zack rattled off a list of names so long, Rae ran out of fingers to count them on. A handful of wolves had tagged along her first hunt as a member of Twin Moon pack, and the number had doubled the second time around. From the sound of it, there would be even more tonight. Some of them were already trotting to the hills and yipping in anticipation, waiting for the Mistress of the Hunt.

Waiting for her. Rae took a deep breath and found the scent of a destiny fulfilled. She had her mate, her pack, her duty.

Just like the old days, her wolf nodded, *when the huntress led her pack in the chase.*

"No," Zack said, reading her mind. "These are the new days. And you know what?"

"What?"

He kissed her. "Something tells me they're going to be good."

Sneak Peek I: Desert Moon

Thank you for reading *Desert Hunt!* Turn the page for a sneak peek of *Desert Moon*, the next book in the series. In it, you'll get to see more of Zack and Rae, in addition to watching Ty find his destined mate and meeting other characters who will get their own love stories in later books of this series. Can you already guess who they are?

Lana Dixon knows well enough to steer clear of alpha males, but Ty Hawthorne is as impossible to avoid as the sizzling Arizona sun. Her inner wolf just won't give up on the alpha who's tall, dark, and more than a little dangerous. One midnight romp under the full moon is enough for Lana to know she'll risk her life for him — but what about her pride?

Ty puts duty above everything — even the overwhelming instinct that says Lana's the one. She's the Juliet to his Romeo: forbidden. And with a pack of poaching rogues closing in, it's hardly the time to yield to his desires. Or is love just what this lonely alpha needs to set his spirit free?

Sneak Peek II: Desert Moon

Chapter One

Lana fidgeted next to her grandmother as the plane banked over the harsh landscape and slowly descended. *Arizona.* She almost muttered it aloud. She'd vowed never to return, and yet here she was.

The desert. All that open space, that sky. It had taken something out of her on her first visit, long ago, leaving her with a thirst she could never quench. So why go back?

The plane landed, and she moved stiffly to baggage claim, already wishing for a flight home. Catching herself grinding her teeth, she willed her jaws to relax. She would be calm and serene, damn it, even if she had to fake it. For one week, she could manage that much. She'd get her grandmother settled into her new home and then return to the East Coast. The desert had nothing for her.

She glued on a smile as an older woman hugged her grandmother, then turned to her with sparkling eyes and a secret smile.

"Lana, you look just like your mother!"

She gave a little internal sigh but didn't drop the forced smile. This must be Jean, her grandmother's old friend. She'd met Jean once before, but her memories of that time were hazy. All she remembered was the sense of loss her first visit had left her with. Which was crazy, because how could you lose something you never had?

"The eyes of her mother, the nose of her father," her grandmother winked, and Lana couldn't help but wonder what private joke they were sharing. But the older women breezed right over the subject and started chatting away about friends and family and times gone by. Lana tapped her foot, waiting for the baggage to roll past. The sooner she got this visit started, the sooner it would be over.

Twenty minutes later, she wheeled the luggage cart toward the exit, trailed by the older women. She sucked in a deep breath before stepping into the furnace outside the airport doors. The heat smothered her like a wool blanket, and the dry desert air seared her nostrils.

"One of Tyrone's boys is coming to get us," Jean said, looking up and down the road.

Lana looked too, gnawing her lip. It figured the kid would be late. While the two older women stood in the shade of a bus stop, catching up on twelve years of news, she paced. Out into the piercing sun, then back into the muted shade. Out and back, out and back again, each footfall a step into the past, then a determined about-face into the future. She tried to numb her senses, but they kept darting around, tasting the arid flavor of this place, listening to its emptiness. Everything felt so familiar, yet so strange, like visiting a childhood home after someone else had moved in.

That was the strange part. Arizona had never been her home and it never would be. She'd only visited once before. She went stiff at the memory, as if the old emotions might creep up and carry her away. Emotions like hope and love and unexpected passion, blazing bright. She'd been so young and impressionable back then — only twenty, and that was the problem. Too young to know better than to fall in love with a vague scent in the hills. For a while, she'd even imagined the scent came with a man.

But it had been a siren song at best, and it had ruined her. There was no man, no promise, only a ceaseless whisper that stirred her during the day and haunted her at night. And now she was back again, right in the thick of it: the heat, the dust, the lying air.

"Oh, there he is," Jean called.

A faded Jeep Wagoneer pulled up to the curb and creaked to a stop. From what Jean had said, Lana had been expecting the driver to be a newly licensed teen — a kid delighted for any excuse to get out on four wheels. The type with narrow shoulders, a pocked complexion, and gangly limbs.

She was not expecting *this*.

Lana gaped as the "boy" emerged from the car with a smooth, easy step. Evidently the state of Arizona was now issuing driver's licenses to rugged, six-foot-two slabs of muscle and raw power. Authority bristled off him in waves, as if he were facing an entire platoon and not just a couple of guests. Dark. Sensual. More than a little dangerous. This was their ride?

"Hello, sweetie." Old Jean gave him a cheery peck on the cheek. The gesture made Lana's inner wolf hiss so fiercely that she wobbled and took a step back. Since when did a man affect her like that?

Since right now, apparently.

But why? She didn't want or need a man in her life, especially one who was so...so...alpha.

And yet every molecule in her body was screaming *Mine!*

∞∞∞

Get your copy of *Desert Moon* to read what happens next! There's a beautiful howling-at-the-moon scene many fans rave about, along with action, drama, and red-hot passion as Ty and Lana fight for their rightful place together as destined mates.

Other books by Anna Lowe

The Wolves of Twin Moon Ranch

Desert Hunt (the Prequel)

Desert Moon (Book 1)

Desert Wolf 1 (a short story)

Desert Wolf 2 (a short story)

Desert Wolf 3 (a short story)

Desert Blood (Book 2)

Desert Fate (Book 3)

Desert Heart (Book 4)

Happily Mated After (a short story)

Desert Yule (a short story)

Desert Rose (Book 5)

Desert Roots (Book 6)

Serendipity Adventure Romance

Off the Charts

Uncharted

Entangled

Windswept

Adrift

Travel Romance

Veiled Fantasies

Island Fantasies

visit www.annalowebooks.com

More from Anna Lowe

Check out the other side of Anna Lowe with a series even die-hard paranormal fans rave about: the Serendipity Adventure Romance series. You can try it FREE with *Off The Charts*, a short story prequel you can receive for FREE by signing up for Anna Lowe's newsletter at *annalowebooks.com*!

Listen to what a few Twin Moon fans have to say about this new series:

- *This is as HOT as her shifter series. For those who want spicy without paranormal, this is a perfect start. I can't wait to read more about these characters.*

- *I'm enjoying Anna's new series just as much as I do her Wolves of Twin Moon Ranch series.*

- *It's not my normal genre but I do love Anna Lowe's romance books because of the great way she writes. I am really happy this book was the same great style.*

- *Uncharted is different from Anna's Wolves of Twin Moon Ranch but I enjoyed the story just as well.*

About the Author

USA Today and Amazon bestselling author Anna Lowe loves putting the "hero" back into heroine and letting location ignite a passionate romance. She likes a heroine who is independent, intelligent, and imperfect – a woman who is doing just fine on her own. But give the heroine a good man – not to mention a chance to overcome her own inhibitions – and she'll never turn down the chance for adventure, nor shy away from danger.

Anna is a middle school teacher who loves dogs, sports, and travel – and letting those inspire her fiction. Once upon a time, she was a long-distance triathlete and soccer player. Nowadays, she finds her balance with yoga, writing, and family time with her husband and young children.

On any given weekend, you might find her hiking in the mountains or hunched over her laptop, working on her latest story. Either way, the day will end with a chunk of dark chocolate and a good read.

Visit AnnaLoweBooks.com

Printed in Great Britain
by Amazon